The Fortune
of Carmen Navarro

The Fortune
of Carmen Navarro

Best wishes from —

jen bryant

EMBER

Text copyright © 2010 by Jennifer Bryant
Cover photographs copyright © 2010 by Shutterstock

Visit us on the Web! www.randomhouse.com/teens

Educators and librarians, for a variety of teaching tools, visit us at www.randomhouse.com/teachers

The Library of Congress has cataloged the hardcover edition of this work as follows:
Bryant, Jennifer.
The fortune of Carmen Navarro / Jen Bryant.
p. cm.
Summary: In this modern-day resetting of the story on which the opera Carmen was based, four teens tell of half-gypsy Carmen, who believes she will become a famous singer, military cadet Ryan's passion for her, and their best friends' efforts to protect them both.
ISBN 978-0-375-85759-1 (trade) — ISBN 978-0-375-95759-8 (lib. bdg.) — ISBN 978-0-375-89546-3 (ebook)
[1. Interpersonal relations—Fiction. 2. Singers—Fiction. 3. Military cadets—Fiction. 4. Romanies—Fiction. 5. Fortune telling—Fiction. 6. Pennsylvania—Fiction.] I. Mérimée, Prosper, 1803–1870. Carmen. II. Title.
PZ7.B8393For 2010
[Fic]—dc22
2009043240

ISBN 978-0-375-85097-4 (pbk.)

RL: 6.0

Printed in the United States of America

10 9 8 7 6 5 4 3 2 1

First Ember Edition 2011

Random House Children's Books supports the First Amendment and celebrates the right to read.

To my editors, Joan and Allison,
with deepest gratitude

Part 1

The world is a ladder on which some go up

and others go down.

☙ *Gypsy proverb*

WILL

We have the whole afternoon off—no drills, no guard duty, no practice, no parades. Free. So Ryan and me, we decide to get lunch at the convenience store and then walk around town—maybe see a movie or take the bus up to the King of Prussia Mall.

We're not even fifty paces from the Academy's front gate, and already Ryan's telling me how he's got to put in extra time on Sunday at the library so he can ace his American history test. Well, I'm in that class and I have that same test, but you won't find me in the library on Sunday. No way. I'll be shooting hoops in the gym or trying to find some poor plebe who'll stand guard for me on Monday so I can smuggle in some cigarettes from Paulie the janitor. Paulie's leaving after next week, and that's a problem for me, see, 'cause I've built up quite a good business among the cadets; some of them'll pay me big bucks for a carton of Marlboros. It's my one little rebellion against the good ol' Valley Forge Military Academy, or the V, as we like to call it. Everything else, I pretty much go along. But no Paulie—no contraband. Not sure what my plan is after he leaves. I may have to shut things down until I can find another supplier.

Anyway, I'm thinking about this, and Ryan's rattling on about how he needs to score at least a 95 on this test to keep his GPA above a 3.8. Yeah, that's right—a three-*eight* . . . as in w*eight* of the world (which is what he always looks like he's carrying before the end of the semester arrives and that report card gets mailed home to Papa Sweeney); as in h*ate* to tell you, Ry, in two years it won't matter a lick what you get on this test or on your report card, and in the meantime, you could be enjoying your life a whole lot more. But, whatever. Back home in Springfield, I'd spent enough time around his old man to know that imperfection was not an option for Ryan. So I try to listen as he rattles off his Sunday study schedule, figuring it's the least I can do for my best friend.

We get to the convenience store around one-thirty and go right to the deli, hungry for anything that doesn't taste like it's been made for a military-school cafeteria. We place our order at the sandwich counter, and kind of at the same time, we notice the girl behind the register up front. Actually, what I notice first—and I'm pretty sure I can speak for Ryan here, too—is her shirt: a tight blue T-shirt with THE GYPSY LOVERS in bold red print across her chest, the *S* letters in the shape of snakes. Everyone else in the place is wearing these dull maroon-collared jobs, little plastic name tags pinned over their hearts. So I figure she's either the store manager or the resident rebel (and since she's looking way too young to be manager material, I'm betting the second). She's hot all right. A sight for sore eyes, especially if your eyes are used to looking at textbooks and military cadets.

I decide I need a better angle. I go behind the snack island and find a good spot between the potato chips and the rows of different-flavored Gatorades, and as I'm walking around the end of the display, I come face to face with Ryan. He pretends he's just looking through the snacks, too, but hey—even shy guys like Ryan have eyes. I poke him and tilt my head toward the front counter. "Nice, huh?"

Ryan turns red and shrugs. The girl at the sandwich counter calls us back for our orders, and then she's yelling something in Spanish that makes Gypsy—her dark eyes dancing and her perfect mouth stretched open—laugh out loud. I glance over at Ryan, who is still blushing and seems unable to move his feet. I grab his arm and we go over to get our lunches, then up to the front, where Gypsy waits to ring us up.

"Hey there, soldiers," she says, flicking her hair off her shoulder and squaring up to face us. "And did we find everything we were looking for today?" Her almond-shaped eyes meet mine directly, not flinching, no hint of shyness.

"Actually . . ." I hesitate, pretending to consider one of the long-stemmed roses in the jar next to the register. I weigh my risk-benefit carefully: Paulie's leaving and I need a new source. Everyone always says I look at least eighteen. The older guy behind the counter (he must be the manager) has moved toward the back. I decide to try: "Carton of Marlboros, please."

She studies me carefully while her hands place our sandwiches in a bag. Behind me, Ryan whispers his warning, but I ignore it. Gypsy's eyes shift to Ryan and she smiles slightly, giving him the once-over. She moves to the other register for a minute, opens the drawer for some change, glances to see if the older guy is still close by. Then she comes back.

"You can get yourself in trouble asking for things that you

shouldn't," she whispers, handing me the bag and my change. She looks again at Ryan, who still seems frozen. "You'd better go eat now," she says, "before he falls over."

"Good idea," I say, thankful that she didn't embarrass me by asking for ID.

I pick up the bag, and as I turn to leave, Gypsy takes one of the long-stemmed roses, leans as far as she can over the counter— and hands it to Ryan.

MAGGIε

They come in through the side door, walk right over to my counter. The tall one, he is good-looking but a little stiff and serious. His friend is more relaxed—not quite as handsome, but cute enough. These military types, they are polite: "One turkey and tomato on wheat with extra mayo; one ham and Swiss on rye, lettuce, brown mustard . . . and could I, please, on that . . . could I get an extra slice of cheese? . . . Great . . . Thanks." (I think at the Academy they must do drills for their manners, too.) So I take down the bread and the knife, I start slicing and slapping on the mayo, the mustard, the cheese. But when I look up to ask if they want onions or peppers (the manager, Frank, he gets angry if we don't ask because it's an extra twenty cents for each), they are gone.

I take a sideways step so I can see between the bins of plastic forks and spoons. . . . Ah, yes, there they are! Two crew cuts and crisp white shirts circling the little snack island in the middle of the store, pretending to pick out their chips and their drinks. But of course, I know what they are really doing: they are looking at Carmen. I see them watching her stack the shelves with cigarettes, flicking her black hair over her shoulders and laughing at something our manager, Fat Frank, is saying.

I go back to making sandwiches, smiling to myself because this is what happens all the time. It is like watching a movie you have already seen before: you know some of the lines and most of the scenes, but still you watch to see what happens. This is because Carmen is the magnet to which guys are drawn like so many pieces of steel. It doesn't matter if they want it to be that way or not. They are drawn. Like bears to honey. Like thirsty travelers to water. Like addicts to a fix. One glance and *boom*—they are hooked!

I wrap the sandwiches, put them on the counter for pickup. "Hey, you two *soldados*! Put your eyes back into your heads and come get your lunch!" But I say that last part in Spanish, and Carmen hears me and laughs, and I think she has already—a girl with eyes in back of her head—checked out both of them. When they go to pay, she flirts with the shorter blond one, and while Frank is not looking, I see her card-dealing trickster hands slip something into his bag. I can see, too, that the tall, serious one, he has already put one foot in her snare.

CARMEN

—◦—

"Rich college kids. Military cadets. Soccer mommies. And a few CPAs who always count their change—that's who your customers will be," the manager, Mr. Ted, told Maggie and me when we were being switched over to the Valley Forge store. "Not like here—men with hard hats and dust on their shoes and little kids saving their dimes for bubble gum," he said, erasing our names from the blackboard in his office. "But you'll do all right there, you two." He handed me my check, smiling at the snake tattoo on my wrist. "No. I don't worry about you."

And now we are two weeks at the Quikmart Valley Forge, and already I can tell you who goes to Villanova (collared shirts, flip-flops—the expensive kind) and who goes to Haverford or Swarthmore (Birkenstocks, faded jeans, *Vegan wrap to go, please*). The accountants have the best silk ties and the nicest watches, and they *do* count their change, *¡ay bendito!* every penny. The mommies in minivans are very tan and always in a hurry. Mostly, they don't even look at me, just jabbering away on their cell phones to the nanny or the husband at the airport and shoving the twenty at me like maybe they have so many they need to get rid of this one quick.

Our new manager, Mr. Frank, he tells us the military academy is only a half mile away, but during our first few shifts, we don't see a single cadet. Then today these two crew cuts come in through the side door looking like naughty puppies who just escaped the leash.

"Always in pairs," Mr. Frank tells me as we restock the shelves above the counter with cigarettes. "It's a rule. Can't leave campus alone unless they get special permission."

I watch them, the two cadets, and I'm thinking they are both kind of cute in their own way, and I'm also thinking that once you are in the military, maybe you always walk a little bit stiff like they do, like there is some invisible drillmaster in your head who counts out *one*-two, *one*-two, *left*-right, *left*-right, even when you are in khakis and buying hoagies at the deli. The taller one, he reminds me a little of Maggie's brother Raúl: dark and serious and a little skinny, but good-looking. He gives Maggie his order, and I see his hands opening and closing like he's not sure—like maybe it's some kind of test and he's thinking something bad will happen if he gets it wrong.

His friend is blond, not so nervous. He thinks I don't see when he goes behind the drink-and-snack display to get a better view of me. But I *do* see and so does Maggie: "Hey, you two *soldados!*" she says. "*¡Pongan los ojos en sus cabezas y tomen su comida!*" And those two Anglos, of course they don't know what Maggie says to them, and this is a good laugh between us.

And then here comes the blond one with the sandwiches and his money and his nice smile all ready. So of course I am not surprised when he asks me for smokes. And of course I know that *he* knows we have video in the store and that he is not eighteen, and there is no way I can let him buy cigarettes with my manager close by putting coins in the safe and filing receipts and those cameras pointed down at the counter. So the blond crew cut and me, we are passing this information back and forth with our eyes when the taller one with the handsome face and nervous hands leans in from behind. "Will, man, don't make her do that," I hear him whisper. "She gives you cigarettes, she gets fired."

Now I am laughing inside because of two things: (1) I can get this boy a hundred cigarettes anytime, and (2) the dark, serious one thinks he's protecting me.

Mr. Frank is still busy with some receipts and I don't think he's really watching us. Just in case, I pretend to make change at the other register, but my hands (that can do a hundred card tricks and make a quarter disappear), my hands do what is needed where the cameras can't see. The whole time, I feel the tall one's eyes on me.

I turn around and give the blond his change and I don't know why—maybe I am thinking of Maggie's brother Raúl, who has always been nice to me—I hand the tall one a rose. I laugh when his handsome face turns as red as the flower in his hand. But then my wrist itches and I know I will see this dark boy again.

WILL

After we leave the Quikmart, Ryan and I walk over to the little town park. We sit at one of the wooden picnic tables, and when I reach into the bag, my hand lands on something small and smooth, about the size of a deck of cards. I look inside and find, slipped in between our sandwiches, a pack of Marlboro Lights.

"Ha!" I laugh, pulling it out for Ryan to see. "Looks like your Gypsy girl likes to bend the rules, too!"

Ryan turns red again when I mention her. He glances over each shoulder, like there are cops in the bushes just waiting to spring on two cadets with sandwiches and a single pack of cigarettes. "How'd she manage that? We were standing right there the whole time. . . ." He puts the rose he's been twirling in his hand on the table between us. "Hey, I'm starving. Hand me mine, will ya?"

I give him his sandwich and take out my own, tearing through the paper in about two seconds and savoring that first bite of real-world food. Ryan unwraps his with the polite precision he's learned from years in the Sweeney household: left side, right side, top, bottom; carefully replace the little bits of lettuce spilling out the sides. "Jeez, Ry, just *eat* the thing," I say. "It's not a freakin' flag-folding ceremony!"

We chew in relative silence, with only the sound of some kids laughing on the distant swing set and the steady hum of street traffic. A flock of robins hops over the stretch of grass between us and the street, pausing now and then to cock their heads and pull up worms. The late-March sun feels warm on my shoulders and makes me think of bikinis, beer, and all the fun I'm planning to have this summer.

I take a few big bites and belch freely, loudly, so that even my polite best friend has to laugh. It feels good to be out in the civilian world again. I miss it sometimes, but not as much as I thought I would. I've learned a lot about myself in my two and a half years at the Academy—stuff I never would have learned if I'd gone to a regular public high school. I'd be too busy showing off or goofing off to really master anything. It took me a while, but finally I had to admit it: I needed the structure of the military to show me that I really *was* somebody, that I really could be disciplined if I wanted to. My grades are better than average now and I'm the co-captain of the soccer team. I always thought that everyone who went here had to go on to the military, but that's not true. Some of them do, but most of us will go to regular colleges. If I can keep it up for another few months, till the end of my junior year, I should get offers of scholarships to Drexel or Temple—and possibly a full ride.

But hey, there's still that tiny part of me that needs freedom, that needs to know that while the Academy has given me this opportunity, it doesn't *own* me. I slide the cigarettes into my pocket, deciding that I need to keep my contraband business alive a little longer—just till the end of the term. And after today, after that girl sneaked me a pack of Marlboros for no obvious reason other than to see if she could do it—well, maybe I've found my new supplier.

I explore this possibility in my head as I finish my sandwich. I crush the paper in my right hand and toss it—*Martens scores with an effortless toss from midcourt*—into the nearby trash can. Meanwhile, my more serious sidekick's only halfway done. He keeps moving the rose around on the tabletop as if he can't quite figure out where it belongs.

"She liked you, Ry," I say as I search the ground for other bits of trash to use for my improvised game of hoops. "You should go back and talk to her. She was hot!"

The color rises up Ryan's neck and spreads across his face. He smiles, though, and I can see that he's embarrassed, but flattered, too. He swallows, puts down the sandwich, and holds up the pack of cigarettes like he's a lawyer displaying evidence in court. "I don't think she's my type, Will," he says, tossing the pack at my chest.

I catch it with one hand; with the other, I snatch the rose from the table and press it to my cheek. "Oh, soldier boy!" I say, standing up and raising my voice as high as I can. "May I shine your boots? Polish your buckle? Rub your rifle? . . ."

Ryan lunges for me, but I anticipate him and shift my weight suddenly to the left. He clutches air. Laughing hysterically, I take off across the grass, my legs churning beneath me, Ryan close behind. We run two full laps around the park before I let him catch me. I'm still laughing when he pins me down in a half nelson beside the empty tennis court.

"OK, OK—I surrender!" I manage to say with the side of my mouth that isn't in the dirt. Ryan loosens his grip. We stand, brush ourselves off. Walking back toward the table, I realize I'm relieved that Ryan still has some spontaneity, that every once in a while, we can still go back to those days in the neighborhood when we didn't have to pass inspection or answer to rank, when our every move wasn't watched and evaluated. On campus, Ryan's usually so uptight that I sometimes find myself wondering if he's the same guy I grew up fishing and playing street hockey with.

"Hey, what the . . . !" Ryan shouts as we get back to the picnic area, just in time to see a raven taking off into the trees with the rest of his sandwich.

RYAN

Why did she do that?

I mean, it's pretty obvious that Will is more her type. He's always been more social. But this incredibly beautiful girl with some kind of strange snake-and-Gypsy logo scrawled across her chest—this girl with the blackest hair and deepest green eyes I've ever seen—this girl who has the guts to slip a pack of Marlboros into our bag with her potbellied boss less than ten feet away and cameras pointed down at the counter—this girl who probably has guys following her like dogs every time she steps out of her house—this girl I can't seem to stop picturing, stop hearing, stop thinking about—this girl who leaned across the counter and looked right through me like she'd known me my whole life—this girl who plucked a single rose from the jar and offered it to *me*—this girl.

Why did she do that?

MAGGIE

What's it like to have such a best friend? Am I jealous? Do I envy Carmen's beauty, her power over men?

Claro. Of course! Only a fool would not want some of that—and Maggie Ruíz is no fool. But things are never as simple as they seem—this much I know, even at sixteen. See, Carmen and me, we have been best friends since forever, since before we could even say a full sentence. We are like *hermanas*—sisters.

My mother, she tells it like this: One day when I am just a *chiquita* and my brothers, Raúl, Carlos, and Marco, are already all day in school, this shabby green van rolls up across the street. A beautiful young woman with a long red skirt and black hair to her waist gets out, and my mother, she sees that the woman is holding a little girl who is screaming at the top of her little lungs and pulling at the woman's hair with her two little hands. The woman runs up the steps and bangs on the door of Señor and Señora Navarro, the old couple from the mountains of Spain who live across from us. Señor Navarro answers, lets them in.

For the rest of the day, my mother says, there is shouting and screaming and the little one crying, and then the van leaves with the sun and it's quiet again.

The beautiful woman never comes back. The little girl stays with the old couple. That same week, Señora Navarro brings the girl over to play and tells my mother that the long-haired lady with the red skirt was her daughter and this is her granddaughter, who must now stay with them forever because the mother can't take care of her. (My mother, she doesn't want to be rude and ask why, so she never does. But later she tells me she thinks the woman was very young and very spirited and that it was probably better for the little girl anyway. "The Navarro couple, they came here a long time ago from the old country, where they grew up as Gypsies. They settled down here, OK, but I think the daughter, she had too much Gypsy blood . . . she had to go.") My mother says as soon as Señora Navarro puts Carmen down on the rug, we are playing together like we do this every day. She says that every morning after, I am running to our front window to wait for Carmen. "Like sisters, inseparable," my mother says.

Elementary school, middle school, and even high school it was like that: sisters, inseparable. It was like that even though anyone could see, as we grew from little girls into young women, which one of us the gods had favored: Carmen, with her sleek black hair, smooth olive skin, and green eyes that made the boys go crazy the minute they saw her. And that should have been enough to turn heads, but no, wait, those crazy gods said: *Carmen, you get more!* I think maybe they felt sorry for her—abandoned by her mother and living in a run-down house with grandparents who were old and too poor to fix their sagging porch and their cracked windowpanes. So Carmen gets a slim waist and just enough bust and hips to make her curvy, but still she can outrun most of the boys on our street. Even in high school she was climbing trees and throwing a baseball as hard and as accurate as any of my brothers.

And what did those crazy gods give me? Well . . . I am not ugly. No, not that. The gods were not cruel, just a little lazy. I am what you call *una muchacha simple.* My hair is thin and brown, and my skin not so smooth, but not too bad. Plain brown eyes and plain mouth. My waist is slim like hers, but so is everything else, so I am still waiting for my curves at sixteen, and now I'm thinking maybe I will be like my aunt Teresa, who waited all her life for a chest that never came and hips that did, but too wide and overnight like Federal Express.

WILL

Ryan and me, this is the third year we've been roommates at Valley Forge. And they've been pretty good years, too. I mean . . . I wasn't so sure about this place at first. Even though I said I'd come here, I didn't expect to like it all that much. But for Ryan, this place was a foregone conclusion. His whole family's military: his dad, his uncle Pete, his brother, Adam—all VFMA grads. All gun-toting, flag-waving patriots.

Me, I don't have any military history in my family—unless, of course, you count my great-great-great-grandfather Thaddeus. He supposedly marched all the way from his farm in Schenectady to Washington, DC, to join the Army of the Potomac, and then (talk about friggin' bad luck) the day after he signed up, he caught yellow fever and died in a makeshift hospital. Never saw a battle except the one he lost to sickness. Helluva legacy, right?

I moved here from New Jersey with my mom and sisters right after my parents split. I was in third grade, and Ryan's been my best friend ever since. We rode the bus together to elementary school, shot hoops almost every afternoon in my driveway, fished together at the reservoir, took karate lessons at the Y. I thought that would all change after sixth grade, when he went to Charlestown Prep and I went to public school in Spring-field. But it didn't. Ryan was still Ryan—just in a uniform and on a different bus. After school and on weekends, he hung out with the rest of us, just like he always had.

Then one day toward the end of eighth grade: "I signed you up for a tour of VFMA," he tells me as we're dragging home the goal cage after an hour of street hockey.

"What for?" I ask.

He laughs. "'Cause I'm going there for high school and I figure maybe you should go there, too."

Now it's my turn to laugh. "Yeah, right, Ry. That swanky place for—" and then I stop. I was gonna say "rich prep-school boys," which was what I'd heard, but Ryan doesn't fit that mold. Even though he went to a private school, he isn't that rich . . . he just had the bad luck of being born into a family that slept, ate, and breathed the military. "Isn't that where they filmed that movie *Taps*?"

"Yeah, that's the one. They made it back in the eighties. Tom Cruise played the renegade. He and Sean Penn were about our age then, I think. . . ."

"Adam went there, too, right?" We are halfway down the block now, dragging the net between us. At the mention of his older brother, Ryan drops the ball and slams it with the stick into the highest point of the curb. Adam is on his second tour in Iraq, and even though his father brags about it every chance he gets, Ryan never mentions it.

"Yeah—and so did my old man."

The ball rolls back to me and I chip it over Mr. Slaymaker's

mailbox, then pick up my dribble on the other side. We continue
down the hill toward Welsh Lane, where our houses face each
other—his freshly painted blue with white trim, ours redbrick
with faded green shutters and my mom's rusty Ford parked half
on the lawn, half on the cracked blacktop drive. At the corner, we
both let go of the net, letting it rest against the curb.

"So you're serious about me visiting the school?"

Ryan stops. He exhales heavily and faces me.

"Yeah, I am. I mean, it's your life—you gotta decide what's
right for you." Over his left shoulder, I can see the neat row of
perfectly manicured boxwoods lined up obediently next to his
family's garage. "But me . . . I don't have much choice. I'm a
Sweeney man, and that's what Sweeney men do." I can't tell if he
is OK with this or not. Old Man Sweeney isn't one to be argued
with; Ryan's been brought up to keep his opinions to himself. "So
I figured you might wanna go, too—you know, be roommates,
twirl rifles, ride ponies, win medals . . . that kind of thing." He
grins. "Besides, chicks dig a man in uniform, and I know *that* part
interests you."

We keep walking past our houses, toward the lot at the other
end of the development. "My dad already talked with your mom.
He can get you a big break on the tuition 'cause of his connections.
He says you'd be a shoo-in for the soccer team and maybe
wrestling, too."

He waits for me to say something—but I don't. Part of me
feels proud that Ryan wants me to come to boarding school with
him. But part of me is pissed that all this has already gone on
without me having a clue.

We get to the lot, drop our gear, and start heaving pebbles from the gravel drive through one of the window frames of the unfinished house. I've got on a loose hooded sweatshirt that my sister (in a rare moment of charity) bought me at a Flyers game her boyfriend had taken her to. Ryan, who played goalie this afternoon, still has on his private-school jacket with the raised gold crest. He piles up some of the larger stones, then unzips his jacket so he can throw better.

We stand side by side, tossing. Me, I'm sharpening my aim—testing my arm from different angles, trying to see how the stones move if I throw them underhand or sidearm or like a knuckleball pitch. But mostly, I'm just goofing off, figuring this is a fun way to kill time outside before dinner, a few pages of algebra, and some TV reruns.

For Ryan, though, it's like there's some invisible enemy standing up there in that window. Someone who's done him wrong and now it's payback time. After a while, I stop throwing and just watch. He's rearing back and heaving the stones through the opening with all his might, each throw a little harder than the one before. After about ten minutes of this, he takes off his jacket and hurls about a dozen more, with no letup in his intensity.

"So, OK, then?" he asks me when he finally quits. There's sweat dripping off his forehead and he's breathing hard. "We leave here Saturday, about one o'clock."

I shrug. "OK—but if I don't like it, I'm not goin' there. Even if it's free."

We pick up our gear and head back to our separate houses.

RYAN

Guilty. That's how I felt at first when I dragged Will to VFMA with me. Well, OK, not *dragged*, exactly—I mean . . . he *said* he wanted to go. It's just that I knew—from visiting my older brother, Adam, when he was a cadet and hearing my dad and my uncle Pete tell stories from when they went—that while you gained some things at the Academy, you also gave some up: No more street hockey. No more sleeping in on Saturdays, eating cold pizza, then biking to the reservoir to fish. No more Sunday afternoons watching Eagles games or lying around in Will's basement listening to Dave Matthews and flipping through the few girlie magazines I'd found buried at the bottom of Adam's desk drawer.

Girls. That's what Will missed the most our first year here. He has an easy way with women that makes them want to stick around. Back home, he was always taking someone to the movies or hanging out with a whole group of them at football games. Even his older sister's friends used to flirt with him. Me, I was just as interested in the female species as he was, but I could never relax enough around them, especially the ones I liked. I tried, but it was no use. I just froze and turned red. And then eventually, after saying something stupid or saying nothing at all, I'd just walk away.

But there are no girls at the V. That's right: None. Zero. Zip.

And even though most of the girls in my class at Charlestown Prep weren't that great, at least we *had* a few. But the Academy high school is all male, and let me tell you, even for a guy like me who's not exactly Mr. Smooth, it takes some getting used to. Once in a while, we actually glimpse a few of the women enrolled at the two-year military college up the hill, but the two schools are entirely separate, so the women might as well be in Egypt or Australia. There's one lady librarian here who's probably under thirty-five, and two English teachers in their fifties . . . but besides them, we have to leave campus and go to the mall or walk into town to see any females.

Starting last year, though, we had to get dates for the Academy dances. I invited a girl I knew from the neighborhood, Lauren Gudel. I hadn't seen her since elementary school, but then I went home for Christmas and we sat in the same pew at church. During the sermon, I couldn't stop glancing sideways at those long legs, that short skirt and tight white sweater. She was hot, all right.

Later, it wasn't hard to talk to her, I guess 'cause our parents have been friends for years and we knew a lot about each other. So I asked her to the New Year's dance, then to the spring formal, and it wasn't too bad. I mean, I didn't feel as nervous as I thought I would; I even kind of enjoyed myself.

I wouldn't say we're serious or anything . . . I mean, I have her picture in my wallet, and we keep in touch online and stuff. Her more than me, though. I don't like to take a lot of time from my studies. I figure as long as I'm expected to be a military man, I might as well aim for West Point and be a leader—spend my life *giving* orders instead of taking them. That would be way too much like home.

WILL

Whenever I pass the little room in the Academy library, I think back to my first campus visit. The Sweeneys picked my mom and me up in their blue Buick and drove us north on Route 202 to the exit at Valley Forge. I'd been in the general area dozens of times before, but usually it was with a friend to go to the movies or to walk around the King of Prussia Mall. I'd never noticed the little blue and white sign next to the exit that said VFMA—3 MILES.

The Valley Forge Military Academy was basically a bunch of plain-looking brick buildings and a big, open area I assumed was the parade grounds. Of course, there wasn't a piece of litter in sight, and the trees looked like they'd been there since Columbus. I'd expected it to look more like a prison, I guess, but it wasn't like that at all—more like a small college campus with all the students walking around in uniform. I kind of liked it.

There were about fifty families visiting that day, and after the headmaster, General Hirshman, talked to us in the auditorium, we split up to take the official tour—dorms, mess hall, gym, chapel, parade grounds, library—then back to the auditorium for refreshments. We skipped that last part, though. Instead, while the moms mingled over lemonade and cookies and met some of the instructors, Ryan's dad led us back over to the library.

"I want to show you boys something," Colonel Sweeney said as we followed him to a small side-room marked ARCHIVES. He ran his fingers along the spines of the yearbooks lining a shelf and pulled one out. After checking the index, he flipped back to the page he wanted and handed the book to us.

Ryan and I looked at the photograph, read the caption: "General John Cooper and Vice President Spiro Agnew congratulate Michael Sweeney and Robert Connell III, the top cadets of the Class of 1973. Both men will be entering West Point in the fall."

There was an uncomfortable silence for a while. You could almost see Ryan's shoulders sag with the weight of his father's legacy. I felt bad for Ry—I mean, what could a guy really say? *Gee, Dad, you're the best?* Or . . . *Boy, I hope I turn out just like you?* Me, I was just looking at a photograph, but Ryan, he was looking at his future—or at least the one his father had picked out for him.

"There you are!" A high female voice, which I recognized as Mrs. Sweeney's, broke into the heavy silence. We looked up and saw the moms standing in the doorway, holding cups of lemonade and a few pamphlets they'd collected from the information tables in the auditorium. I felt myself breathe normally again.

"Captain Greene says the boys are welcome up at the training wall if they want. . . ."

One glance at Ryan told me he couldn't wait. He snapped the yearbook closed and handed it back to his old man.

"Cool, Dad. Thanks for showing us that. . . ." He didn't need to ask me if I wanted out of there. He'd known me too long for that. "We're gonna head up to the wall."

While Colonel Sweeney slipped the yearbook back on the shelf, I followed Ryan as he walked quickly toward the library door, his clenched fists swinging at his sides.

RYAN

Once we knew we were in, my dad pulled some strings so Will and I could room together. That first year was a big adjustment for us both, but at least I knew what we were in for; Will had no idea. Even so, he took to all the rules and the strict daily routine a lot quicker than I thought he would: up at six, dress, inspection, breakfast, class, lunch, class, drill, athletic training, shower, dinner, study, inspection, lights out at ten o'clock.

Sharp.

If we couldn't sleep, we'd talk about the Eagles or the Phillies or the 76ers, depending on what season it was. Sometimes we'd talk about our families, too.

Will told me that the main reason his parents split up was that his dad had a gambling problem. "My old man made pretty good cash as an engineer at GE, but then he'd wind up at the track or at some high-stakes poker game and blow it all," he explained. "He kept promising my mom that he'd stop, but I don't think he could. Once, he lost his car at some sleazy poker joint and had to call our neighbor to bring him home. When Mom found out, she called the divorce lawyer the next morning."

That explained a lot. Even though Will isn't a problem gambler, he loves to see what he can get away with. And even though he seems to follow the rules like most everyone else at VFMA, he's always on the lookout for a little breathing room, a little hole in the fence that he can slip through without anyone noticing. Last year, he made a connection with someone up at the college: the guy would come down about every two weeks with a stack of pirated DVDs, which Will distributed through the dorm for five bucks apiece.

The guys would watch them at night on their PCs or in the library at one of the desks in the back. Nothing X-rated—just regular movies. It was harmless enough.

Then this year, he makes a deal with one of the linen delivery guys to smuggle in cigarettes. That goes even better for him till one of the younger cadets, Jake Nash, gets caught behind the gym with a fresh carton of Lucky Strikes. Jake doesn't give Will up, but the delivery guy gets scared and says he doesn't want to lose his job over "a bunch of kid soldiers."

I think maybe that's the end of it, but then Paulie the janitor provides another opportunity. Will watches him for several weeks around campus before he approaches him with his offer: Will plans to collect cash from the cadets who want cigarettes, and Paulie will deliver them in an unmarked box that he'll leave in the janitor's closet behind the gym. They'll split profits fifty-fifty.

But because of the close call with Jake, Will asks for my approval. "I want you to know exactly what I'm doing with Paulie.

You got me in here, and God knows what I'd be into if I was still out there." He nods his head toward the front gate, where, on the other side, there are people wearing cutoffs and flip-flops and deciding for themselves where and when to eat and whether they'll be fitting in a visit to the gym, hanging out with friends, or spending the evening on the couch with a bag of Cheetos and *Law & Order* reruns.

"This is just business, plain and simple—a little goodwill for the guys and a little pocket change for yours truly." He grins that grin that would make the neighborhood girls swoon. "But, Ry, if it's gonna get you into trouble—if you say Hey, don't do this—then I won't."

I think about it. For three days, I think about it. And during those three days, I realize something: I envy Will's freedom. I envy his fatherless, working-class home life that makes him believe he has absolutely nothing to lose. If Will screws up, well . . . it's temporary. A human flaw, a misstep. Who's really gonna care? His tired mom, who couldn't stop thanking and hugging my father the day Will decided to come here? His old man, whose picture probably illustrates the dictionary under "addiction" and "irresponsible"? I don't think so. For three days, I can't stop wondering what it must feel like to be Will Martens—no pressure to get straight As; no expectation to carry on the family legacy; no pacing, frowning, hour-long lecture from the colonel every time you somehow "disappoint" him. God . . . what *would* that be like?

On the morning of the fourth day, I wake up early and can't get back to sleep. I get up and go for a slow jog around the campus.

When I get back to our room, Will has left for breakfast at the mess hall. I towel off and leave this note on his desk: *About your plan—go for it.* And for a minute, I actually think about leaving him a twenty, saying, *Count me in.* But then—I don't. Gathering my books, I walk toward the library to study for the chemistry quiz I am sure we'll be having that morning.

MAGGIE

Carmen can work more hours now because she dropped out of school. Me, I was going to drop out, too, but my mother, she says: "Look, you see these?" and she holds out her hands—small and womanly, but with hard calluses at the base of every finger and blisters on both palms from scrubbing the floors and bathrooms at the Holiday Inn, where she has worked since I was in kindergarten. "You see this?" she says, pulling me over to the kitchen table, where her check for two weeks is barely enough to buy groceries. "No—you will stay in school so your hands, they don't look eighty when you are not yet forty, so your check will be enough for a nice house and car and maybe some left over for a nice dress to wear out to a fancy restaurant." And she turns away quick.

So the next day, I go to the office of my counselor at school and we look at my grades. She asks me lots of questions about what I like and what I already know how to do and what I think I might be interested in. And somewhere in there, I tell her about the stray dog that wandered into our yard, the one I let sleep under our porch while I healed his bloody paws and fed him until his ribs no longer poked through his thick black fur. I tell her how I think I might have a gift for healing and maybe I might like to work in an animal hospital, and by the time I leave school that day, I am enrolled in the Applied Sciences program at the vocational school.

I try to get Carmen to sign up, too, but no use. There is no making Carmen do something she doesn't want to do. *De nada sirve*. It's not worth it, like spitting into the wind. Besides, she has her dreams, and who am I to spoil them? "I am going to be a famous singer who will travel across the country in a tour bus." That's what she told me. That's why she left high school as soon as she could and why she stays up late at night writing lyrics for her songs and practicing her guitar in the basement. It's true that her voice is beautiful. It's true that when her band, the Gypsy Lovers, plays at Gallagher's, the pub is so packed they have to hire guys to stand at the door for crowd control. So who knows? Maybe she will make it big in the music business.

Last week, when we are at the mall, I help Carmen pick out a new outfit for the stage. We get to the register, and she has the red silk shirt and short black skirt and shiny candelabra earrings to catch the lights. Then I see she also has the pair of gold hoop earrings that I had in my hand before but don't have the money to buy.

"Hey—what are you doing?" I say when I see her paying the clerk, but too late and now I am the owner of these earrings.

Three times I try to give her the money I have with me, but she says: "No, Maggie. You keep your money for college. . . . I will sing like a bird for some years and then I will grow old and alone and you will have your good job and a husband and family and then I will come knocking on your door and you will have to take me in." And as soon as she says this, I laugh at this idea of my perfect, invincible sister needing a home and someone to love her.

But Carmen, she does not laugh.

CARMEN

Almost everyone who walks in here has a good job, a nice car, an education. It's not like the Quikmart back in Norristown, where Maggie and me worked before. Not at all.

But you know what I think? Even people with straight teeth and expensive clothes who go to college or work in lawyers' offices—even they have worries and longings and broken hearts. When they pass through the line at lunchtime or at night on the way to the tennis club or yoga class, I listen to their arguments and conversations, their tired sighs, their complaints and flirtations. This is all good material for my lyrics.

You see this little notebook here, the one with coffee stains and the red ribbon to mark my place? I bring it with me to work and keep it below the counter. Whenever I get a break, I write down a few lines—maybe something one of the soccer mommies said, or some detail about a rich guy's tie, or maybe the look on that shy cadet's face when his friend asks me for cigarettes.

Then at home again, when *mis abuelos* are asleep in their bed, I drink a mug of strong coffee and slip into the basement with my guitar. I sit on the old green couch and I try to remember my mother's voice. Abuelita, she does not talk about my mother, but one time she says: "Your mother had a beautiful voice and she would sing like a bird when she was happy." So I remember this—and I use it. My one connection to her. I think about my mother's voice and I strum a few chords. I read over the pages in my notebook. I sing the lines I have written, then I switch them around. I listen for a melody, for something that makes a good refrain. Sometimes I am there for two, three, four hours and nothing good happens. I play more chords, I try this melody and that one. I try again. Nothing.

But sometimes I can spin a whole song from one little thing, and then when I find just the right rhythm, just the right notes— *aah!* It's like when you are playing poker and the dealer hands you a royal flush, or when you are walking home and you smell the wind and you know that it will rain hard in exactly two minutes and you run inside just in time.

It is like offering a flower to a shy boy and knowing for certain that he will think of you day and night until he sees you again. It is a gift. A power like magic—Gypsy magic.

I have it.

Part 2

When that girl laughed . . . there was no talking sensibly.

Everyone laughed with her.

Prosper Mérimée, CARMEN

MAGGIε

—◦❦◦—

Come to the cave after dinner. This is the message I get from Carmen, who almost never texts me but instead walks out on the porch or throws open her bedroom window and yells across the street: "Hey, Maggeeeeee!" So now I am rushing to finish the left-over beans I heated up to eat at my desk, trying not to spill them on my last page of math. I am rushing because I love to spend the evening in the Cave (which is really just the basement of Carmen's house), where we read our fortunes in the cards and flip through magazines, and where there are no big brothers or mothers or *abuelos* to bother us. I am rushing because this is something we don't do so much now that Carmen works more hours and I have to keep up my grades so I can get into the better classes next year and maybe get a scholarship for college. I am rushing because the text means Carmen is in the middle of some-thing she doesn't want to interrupt, and probably it is a new song that she will play for me first and this is always a special time be-tween us, like Christmas.

I finish my meal and open the drawer where I keep the key to Carmen's house that I have had since sixth grade. "You are family, Maggie," Señora Navarro tells me that day as she puts it in my hand, small and shiny and with my name printed on tape on one side. "You come here anytime and eat, sit, visit, rest. . . ." And I say, "*Bueno, gracias,*" but I don't do it. At my house, someone is always coming or going, and doors and windows are more open than closed. But Carmen's grandparents are what you call private people, and I don't feel right just walking into their house like that. So for many months after she gives me the key, I am still knocking at the front door and waiting for someone to come and let me in.

But then another year goes by, and all at once my skinny brothers wake up with biceps and mustaches. They lock the bathroom to shave their faces and are always smelling like beer and cheap cologne. There is always a radio blaring or an engine revving or someone yelling and doors slamming in the hall. All of a sudden my brothers and their friends are everywhere, taking up all the quiet.

One day when I am in eighth grade, it is too much. I grab some paper and a pen and my schoolbooks with pages marked to study for two tests. I slam my own door and walk fast across the street with my key to Carmen's house. I remember letting myself in through the front and sitting down at the table in the quiet kitchen. I remember pouring a glass of water from the hand-painted pitcher that sits on the shelf. I remember memorizing all the parts of a cell and writing a description of animal respiration, and I remember reading every page twice and taking many notes in that house with no brothers and their big voices and engines— just Señor Navarro weeding and hoeing the little garden in the back and Señora Navarro mending socks on the porch. And of course, on those tests I take the next day, I get my first two As of the year, and the teacher uses her red pen on my paper only for writing *Excellent* and drawing a smiley face on the top.

Now I am remembering that night as I walk across the street and let myself in. The Navarro house is just like it was then: *quiet.* I close the door and walk halfway down the hall. At the far end, light flickers on the wall from the TV that is turned way down so that Señor Navarro's snoring is the only sound. I open the basement door to go down the winding wooden stairs that look like so many thin slices of pie.

"Hey! *¿Qué pasó?*" Carmen cries when she sees me. She keeps strumming her guitar and nods for me to sit next to her on the Dragon, which is what we call the green couch we found one day about four blocks away with a crayon sign: FREE—YOU HAUL. And of course we had to stop walking then and sit on those cushions, and Carmen says she had to have this big, ugly couch for her basement because it gives off good energy. And of course I was saying right away that this couch looked heavier than a car and we were too far away from where we live and besides it would never fit in that basement. But if you know Carmen, you know that these words are to her like kerosene on a fire, and now she will have this couch no matter what. So we waited until her grandparents went out, and she begged Marco and Raúl to help us push and pull it to the house and *¡ay· Señor!* up the front steps and through the front door, and we almost crushed my brother's left hand squeezing it down the narrow stairs, but finally there it was in that basement and for good because no one wants to have to move it ever again.

I am remembering this while my eyes get used to the almost-dark of the Cave: only one little lamp and two candles that smell like roses. I move the pile of magazines onto the floor and sit down on the Dragon. Beside me on the cushion, Baji opens one big green eye, flicks her white-tipped tail, then goes back to her cat dreams. Carmen tries a series of chords and then another and another; in between, she is scratching out lines in her notebook and humming a little. I pick up a magazine, adjust the one little lamp, and begin to read about the actress who was seven times in rehab but now she finds Jesus and is sober and wants to be a minister. The article is long, and I am reading to find out if she can really do that when Carmen strums one chord very loud.

"*Ha!* There it is *¡por fin!* You want to hear?" And this is not a real question between us because she already knows the answer. I put the magazine down, even though I really want to know if the actress will someday be a minister or if the number 7 really isn't so lucky.

> *Here you are again,*
> *I knew we'd meet again,*
> *But why so nervous, why so shy . . . my, my!*

> *Let me see you smile, let me take your hand,*
> *Don't be afraid . . . no, no!*
> *You are my darling red-faced boy.*

> *I know what you want, I know what you need,*
> *Take my hand, come with me,*
> *I can take you where you've never been before—*
> *You are my darling red-faced boy.*

I offer you a flower, a red and thornless rose,
You stare at me so longingly, now tell me
I'm the girl you want to know.

Let me see you smile, let me take your hand,
Don't be afraid . . . no, no!
You are my darling red-faced boy.

Halfway through, I am tapping my feet on the floor. In my mind, I see the usual crowd at Gallagher's after the Gypsy Lovers have played this new song: there is whistling and stomping and clapping, and someone who has had too many beers shouts, *Again!*

"What do you think, Maggie? Is it good? *¿Qué te parece?*" And this is not a real question, either, because Carmen can see already that I think it is *very* good.

She tightens one string, plucks, loosens another, then begins the whole thing again. This time, I listen closer to the words. I think of all the boys who have fallen under her spell, every one of them turned into a song—sometimes several songs—before she tires of them and moves on. I remember how embarrassed that tall cadet looked as he left the store, his face almost as red as the rose in his hand.

I smile at my friend who the gods have blessed with beauty and a voice like a bird, my friend whose *mamá* left her one day with no explanation and never returned. That shy cadet—I wonder how many songs he will last.

CARMEN

Like running six blocks in wet shoes and a heavy coat. Like trying to catch a cricket in your kitchen that you can hear but can't see. Like baking a cake that looks perfect, but after two minutes on the shelf, the middle sinks and now you have a big soggy donut. Mostly, that's how it feels to write songs. Note by note, chord by chord, phrase by phrase; cross out, go back. Make a long list of words that rhyme with "heart" or "gone" or "love," but not the ones everybody else uses. Something original—but simple, too. Something you can remember and hum to yourself after the first time you hear it. Something that sticks in your mind like fear . . . or love.

When I leave the store on Saturday, the snake on my wrist still itching and two whole pages of my notebook filled with lines, I know there is a new song for me soon. It will take a little work (*¡Dios mío!* they are never easy!), but I know this song will come quicker than most.

Tonight I play it for Maggie, who has a voice like rusty spoons but a good ear, and always I know she is being honest with me. She likes it right away, I can tell. "What are you calling it?" she asks. " 'Shy,' " I say. And then I see Maggie is not sure about this title. "Sing it again for me," she says, so I do. "That refrain 'red-faced boy,' that is your title," she says. And so that is what it is because Maggie is my sister who is smart and honest and knows some things.

I play this new song two more times after she leaves and I think I like it very much. I let myself dream that I am singing it for ten thousand people in a big arena and everyone in Philadelphia is hearing it on the radio. I picture again the tall cadet with the nervous hands and his friend who is bold enough to ask me for cigarettes, and I wonder what the Fates have planned for us.

I rest my guitar against the Dragon and slip down to the floor with my luckiest deck. I spread the cards facedown in a circle like *abuela* taught me. Closing my eyes, I let the Fates guide my hand. I choose only three, pushing the rest away. First card: the two of hearts (a romance is possible); second card: the eight of diamonds (skill is rewarded); third card: the joker (something unexpected, uncontrolled).

I kiss each of the picked cards, put them back in the deck. I blow out the candles, turn off the lamp, and sit for several minutes in the pitch dark. The air smells of roses. Deep breath . . . cross my heart, *Mother Mary, be with me.*

March 18, 2007
Baghdad, Iraq

Dear Ryan,

   *I guess this damn war must be softening me up
because I don't think of you as my stupid kid brother
anymore. (Nice of me, huh?) But seriously, Mom's letters
say that you are doing them proud at VFMA—making
great grades, getting promoted to cadet captain, leading
the fall debate team—and by the looks of the last photos
she sent, you're staying in top shape, too. Well, good for
you. I just hope you get to use all of your discipline and
talent in the good old US of A and you never have to set
foot in this place.*

   *I thought my second tour over here would be a lot
easier than the first, but now I know how wrong I was
about that. Yeah, I'm used to the noise, the heat, the dust,
the sore feet, and the constant feeling that I'm in the sights
of some hidden sniper or on the hit list of the next suicide
bomber. None of that bothers me much anymore. But
you know what does? The feeling that me and my men
(and there's at least a dozen of us who've gone home and
then had to come back again) are going out on patrol,
risking our necks every second of every day—and
everything about this place is staying exactly the same.
Sure, we see a new building getting finished here and
there or a street made safe that was off-limits to the Iraqi
civilians just a few months before. But for every new*

building, there seems to be two that are blown up, burned down, or just plain abandoned for fear of the insurgents. And for every street made safe, there's at least one more that overnight becomes a scene from some 1960s Western: no people, no vehicles, no open doors or windows—just a hot, dusty quiet and the odd feeling that death waits around the next corner.

Sorry, Ry. I just realized I've been ranting at you. I don't regret joining the military. . . . I love the life, I love my men, my unit, my country. I just don't love this war anymore.

Be good (I know that's so hard for you—ha!),
Adam

PS Write back.
PPS If you talk to Mom, ask her to send me my old football jacket—it gets colder than stone here at night.

WILL

Sometimes I can't believe my good luck. Ryan—who, before we walked into that convenience store, couldn't be persuaded by me or anyone else to skip class, bribe a plebe, or break curfew—is *finally* realizing that there's more to living than medals and uniforms. Ever since that Gypsy chick behind the counter smiled and gave him a rose, it's almost like he's a different person. Yesterday, for example, he was late for parade. (I covered for him, though: I told the sergeant that he'd received an emergency call from home; but actually, he was on the phone with someone at the Quikmart, trying to find out her work schedule.) Then last night, he failed the room inspection that we've all known was coming for over a week. (I couldn't cover for him then.) Had I realized how much that girl had taken over his brain, I would have reminded him. But hey, it's Ryan Sweeney, our cadet captain— Mr. Rulebook, Mr. Super Soldier himself. Who would have thought he'd just plain *forget?*

And here's the good-luck part: A few days ago, I check my campus mailbox and pull out a plain brown envelope. Inside, there's a flattened Lucky Strikes pack. A handwritten note says: *I can get you more of these.* No return address, no signature, nothing to indicate who it's from. But I know right away it's from Gypsy at the convenience store. I don't know how she got my box number, but I like the fact that she did—it means she's clever and has connections.

I hold on to the note. As expected, Paulie the janitor leaves, and the new guy, Sandy, wears a T-shirt that says I SUPPORT THE BOY SCOUTS OF AMERICA. I'm thinking there's not a *real* good chance he'll run contraband, so I decide to give the Quikmart girl a try. On Wednesday, I get permission to ride the truck into town to help Sergeant O'Connor with a load of supplies. I've learned that even the most hard-nosed sergeants look for excuses to linger outside the walls of the Academy, so when I suggest we stop at the Quikmart for donuts and coffee, O'Connor is happy to oblige.

When we arrive, Gypsy is at the register ringing up customers. She recognizes me and smiles. I take my time and stroll through the store, grabbing a bottled iced tea and a candy bar for later, a bag of powdered donuts for the ride back. Pouring myself a large coffee, I wait until the other customers have left. I make sure the sergeant is still busy picking his lottery numbers before I head toward Gypsy.

"And did we find everything we're looking for today?" she asks me innocently as I place my items on the counter. Her eyes, if it's possible, are larger and greener than before. She's wearing the standard store uniform—a drab maroon-collared shirt and black pants—but she still looks pretty hot. Over her heart, a white and black plastic name tag says CARMEN.

"Yes, ma'am, I did," I reply, glancing over to be sure O'Connor is still occupied. "You, uh, have a large inventory here. . . . You must get deliveries pretty frequently." Carmen scans my items and places them in the bag, her snake tattoo slithering as she moves her wrist.

"You have a good eye for business!" she remarks, knotting the top and handing it over to me. As we talk, I'm watching her hands carefully; no surprises for me in this bag, I'm certain.

"Baked goods and dairy every Monday and Wednesday. Drinks and packaged snacks on Thursdays. . . ." Then, ever so subtly, she tips her head toward the cigarettes, a move that swiftly morphs into a tossing back of her raven black hair. "But now I remember: you like our sandwiches, yes? We get our lunch meats every Saturday. You should come by then with your handsome friend," she says, casually straightening the rows of soft pretzels on the counter. "Two o'clock is a very good time to come. . . ."

A well-dressed woman and two kids come up behind me to check out. My nod tells Carmen that I understand. I walk quickly to the door.

Outside in the truck, I wait for Sergeant O'Connor to pay for his lottery tickets. Setting my coffee in the holder between the seats, I reach into the bag and open the donuts. Inside, I find a pack of Winstons. I look up quickly, in total disbelief. *How did she . . . ?* Through the front window of the store, I watch Carmen give the customer her change. When the woman leaves, Carmen turns toward me and shrugs, laughing.

MAGGIε

On Thursday, the boss says OK, Carmen can have the early
shift on Saturday if we both work a longer shift on Sunday and this
is good because the Gypsy Lovers have a gig at Gallagher's Pub
and Carmen will need extra time to get ready.

So now it is Saturday and of course we are both looking
forward to Gallagher's and we are watching very carefully the
clock in the boss's office. And because of this, I am sometimes
forgetting to ask the customers if they want the extras and once I
make a ham and cheese for a soccer mommy who wants meatless
and she complains to Frank, who shakes his fat finger at me and
tells me to pay attention or don't bother coming to work.

It's almost two o'clock when Carmen punches out for the day
and leaves through the back door. Mike, who drives the cigarette
delivery truck for all the Quikmarts around Philadelphia, will
arrive on the hour, and he and Carmen will make arrangements
for the cadet to get a box of cigarettes for a price. Carmen will
make sure it is hidden before she goes home to get dressed, do
her hair, and warm up her voice.

Before, at the other store, they did some of this smuggling
with Mike's cousin who lived down the block and no one ever

found out. That was lucky. Gypsy luck, Carmen says, because two times she was not careful and almost got caught. So when we come to work at this store, I say something to Carmen like maybe this is a good time to stop the deals with Mike. I say that even though it's just a few cartons of cigarettes, that maybe it is still stealing.

And you know what Carmen says? She says Mike the driver, he has five kids and a sick wife and this was his idea in the first place. I say how do you know this for sure, and she says he and his kids are always asking Father Matthew at St. Anne's Catholic Church to pray for the wife. Carmen says she sees them there whenever she takes her *abuela* to Mass. I say OK, but maybe we can find another way to get them money so maybe nobody gets caught and loses their job and maybe even goes to jail.

The next day Carmen asks if we can go look on my computer (her *abuela* has heard of computer viruses and thinks they are evil spirits living inside the machine and this makes her very afraid, so Carmen, she cannot have a computer in that house and has to use mine or the one at the library) and I say OK, but I don't know why. Then Carmen is showing me on three different Web sites how much money the tobacco companies are making this year (about sixteen *billion* dollars) and then she shows me the St. Anne's parish Web site where they are posting photos of people to pray for and Mike the driver's wife is one of them and she is smiling on the couch with her kids but she looks tired and her skin looks too yellow and her bony knees and elbows are poking through her dress that she probably wore before she got sick because now it is three sizes too big. Carmen says she tries to give her share of the money to Mike for the wife but Mike says no deal unless Carmen keeps her share. So Carmen, she sees at the furniture store a handsome recliner for her grandfather and a matching rocker for her grandmother. She puts them on layaway and uses the cigarette money to pay down the cost so it can be a surprise for their anniversary.

So now after I see these numbers on the computer and the picture of the wife, I am what you call an accomplice. I watch to be sure Fat Frank stays inside so Carmen and Mike can do their business outside in the back. And today, when the two cadets walk in and there is our boss at the register and no sign of Carmen, *ay*, you can see their disappointment. They come over to the deli and place their order. I make their sandwiches. I slide Carmen's note inside the wrapping of the tall one's, like she said. I put their lunches up on the counter.

"Thanks. Uh, is your friend here, by any chance?" the shorter one asks. He is very friendly and has an easy smile like you see on guys who make it big in the movies. The tall, shy cadet is standing behind this one, but he is listening, too, I can tell. I take my time, slice open a few rolls. The cadets wait politely.

"She left early today to get ready for something . . . ," I say, noticing how the tall one's shoulders droop when he hears this news. Then, in a lower voice: "I think maybe after you pay, you should go around to the back door and I will show you where to find your other package."

And now there is an "OK, thanks a lot" and another smile from the blond cadet and still the drooping shoulders and no smile from the tall one. But I know this will change soon. I

imagine the look on his handsome face when he unwraps his
lunch and finds the note:

> *To a shy soldier:*
>
> *If you like good music, you should come to Gallagher's
> tonight at nine o'clock. I will look for you there.*
>
>

Carmen
>

RYAN

We take stock of the situation from across the street. The two guys at the door are huge—at least six feet three and two hundred pounds each. They're checking IDs and turning away those who don't have one. In the front window, underneath the stenciled letters GALLAGHER'S PUB, a poster announces:

THE GYPSY LOVERS
Saturday, March 29, 9 p.m.
$8—cover

The line to get in stretches halfway to the corner.

"Now what?" I ask Will. I should have anticipated this. All we have are our VFMA IDs, and I'm pretty sure they're worthless for getting us in.

"C'mon, we can do this," Will says confidently, stepping off the curb and starting across the street before I can protest. I follow, wishing I shared his optimism, but also knowing that if I have to be sneaking into a bar, it's Will I want to be sneaking in with. But before we reach the other side, someone comes up from behind and pushes us to the front of the line.

"These two are good, Charlie," the guy—who is about my height, but has long, dark hair and wears a plain black shirt and leather vest—says to the bouncer as he escorts us through the front door. Will's half-panicked look asks me if I know him; I shake my head in a silent reply.

Inside, it's loud and already pretty crowded. Here and there, my feet stick to the floor where someone has spilled a beer. Our leather-clad savior leads us expertly through the crowd and toward a small table at the far side of the room.

"Carmen sings there," he explains, pointing to the very front of the room, where four microphones and a drum set stand on a makeshift stage. "Band starts at nine—enjoy." He turns and disappears into the crowd.

"That was—um . . . *interesting*," Will says as we arrange two chairs to face the stage. "Who *was* he?"

"Hell if I know," I reply. We sit, breathe. I can feel my heart racing and my palms are damp.

"Maybe your Gypsy girl has a male harem—and you're just the newest member!"

My stomach tightens at Will's suggestion. I know he's just kidding around, but the thought of Carmen being interested in another guy makes me tense—angry, even. I know I'm being stupid. But I can't help it.

I scan the crowd, trying to get my bearings in this strange place. At the Academy, they teach us to assess new situations quickly, to determine, in a split second, whether we're in friendly or enemy territory. This feels like both. On the one hand, there are a lot of young people who are well dressed and fairly orderly.

A few wear T-shirts or hoodies from Villanova, Haverford, Swarthmore, Cabrini. I'll bet that like many of our cadets, they only live around here during school.

But the others look like locals—mostly in their twenties, but some older, maybe in their thirties and forties. Most are huddled in groups around the wooden bar that stretches the length of the room. Three bartenders are working the spigots and bottles, shouting and joking with the customers, wiping the counter, and filling the pretzel bowls.

"So *this* is what the rest of the world does on a Saturday night," Will exclaims, pocketing the matches and a coaster from the stack in the center of the table. "Beats trolling the mall or watching *Top Gun* for the fiftieth time with the plebes."

"Yeah, it's not bad," I agree.

"What'll it be, gents?" A waitress, who's definitely in her forties if she's a day, appears at our table. "We got Miller Lite, Sam Adams, Yuengling, and Coors Light on tap. Any of them suit ya?"

I look over at Will. We both turned seventeen last month—and thanks to our military demeanor, I guess, most people think we're older. Maybe the front door was the only ID check. But maybe not. I shake my head to let him know we can't risk getting thrown out.

"Just two Cokes for us, please," he replies, his shoulders drooped in exasperation.

The waitress shrugs, drops a small plastic bowl of pretzels in front of us, then moves on to the next table.

"You know, Sweeney," Will says, digging into the snacks, "I give up a lot to be your best friend. When we get to the Pearly Gates of Heaven"—he shakes a pretzel close to my face—"God's gonna wave me to the front of the line for all the times I sacrificed for you!" He laughs, though, and I have to laugh, too—picturing Will in line at Heaven's gate, where (for once) his reputation will precede him.

WILL

It'd be pretty easy to convince me to do this just about every weekend. I mean, look: girls, music, and beer. Even though we're not drinking, it still feels like we've been let out of jail for a while. It's awesome, this freedom. You can almost taste it.

As usual, I'm trying to appear supercool to balance out my best friend's anxiety. Ryan's nerves have been on hyperalert ever since that guy shoved us through the entrance. Truth is, even though I dig being here, I'm a little edgy myself. Three reasons: First, we told the on-duty sergeant that we'd be taking the shuttle bus to the King of Prussia Mall and then to the movie theater. If somehow he finds out we've spent the evening at a local bar, we're toast. I'm pretty good at persuasion, but even *I* can't explain us out of this one.

Second, even in casual dress, we stand out in this crowd—everyone else is coupled up guy-girl, or else they're part of a big group of ten, twelve, fifteen people. Then there's the two of us, in neatly pressed collared shirts and khakis. (Why didn't I think to stuff a T-shirt in my pants? At least then we wouldn't look like the Wrigley's Doublemint twins.) We might as well have MILITARY DWEEB stamped on our foreheads.

Third, there's a history of bad blood between VFMA and the local guys—townies, we call them: the ones who are out of high school (one way or another), but who still live and work around here. Most of the time, tensions are confined to four-letter words and sexual slurs hurled at us from cars passing by the Academy. And if we get to the mall on weekend leave, we can usually count on some verbal abuse about our dress or our flattop haircuts or how—even when we try not to—we end up walking the mall in almost perfect one-two synchrony.

Once in a while, though, tensions erupt. Take last October, for example. We'd heard at evening mess that Derek Lyman, a plebe, got separated from his roommate in town and had a run-in with the locals. "They jumped me from behind while Rob was in the shop across the street. They dragged me into an alley and almost tore my arm off!" he told us when we crowded into his dorm room a few hours after it'd happened.

The attack had occurred in broad daylight, just a few yards from the main street, but despite a plea from General Hirshman to the local police, no witnesses stepped forward. Derek healed up eventually, but he missed the entire wrestling season with a broken wrist and a badly dislocated shoulder. After that, we were all pretty careful to stick together off campus.

So now here we are, basically AWOL, and looking about as comfortable as a plebe at his first day's training, and all because that Gypsy girl smiled at Ryan and gave him a rose.

"Here ya go!" our waitress announces, placing a plastic glass of Coke before each of us. "Now, not too many of these if you're driving, boys," she teases, and moves on to the next table.

I resist the urge to say something really rude. Instead, I toss a few pretzels at my best friend.

"I know, I know. I owe you for all your sacrifices . . . Pearly Gates and front of the line and all of that," he admits. Ryan can really frustrate me sometimes—but it's hard to be flat-out *mad* at the guy.

The lights dim and the hundreds of conversations get suddenly quieter. People turn toward the makeshift stage, where a short, balding man is walking toward the center microphone.

"Ladies and gentlemen—thanks so much for coming out tonight. I'm Tommie, the manager here at Gallagher's. We're so glad to have back with us tonight one of the most talented and energetic bands in the Philly area. Please put your hands together and give a warm welcome to . . . the Gypsy Lovers!"

The crowd breaks into thunderous applause as the band members file onto the stage. There are three guys who look like they're in their early twenties, and one of them I recognize right away as the dude who got us in. Then comes Carmen, smiling big and waving to the crowd, looking awesome in a red shirt, short skirt, and high heels, drawing whistles and whoops from the men. I continue clapping as the musicians take their places and adjust their instruments. I glance over at Ryan, who appears mesmerized. He isn't looking around, or sipping his Coke, or anything—I'll bet he hardly knows where he is.

They play their first set, and everyone in the place is really into them. Carmen looks even hotter than she did in the store. And when she sings, I have to admit I am blown away by her voice. My mom used to have these old recordings of a pop singer from the

UK named Sheena Easton. I used to complain about my mom's taste in music, but never about Sheena. She sounded like Stevie Nicks, Tina Turner, and Janis Joplin all rolled into one. Carmen sounds a lot like that: she's incredible. The rest of the band is good, too. Our guardian angel plays lead guitar; he's one of those guys who're so good it's less like he's playing than *becoming* the music. They obviously know how good he is, too, because they let him riff whenever they can.

After their fifth song, I shout over the applause: "You OK?" Ryan hasn't moved a muscle since they started. He nods, but doesn't take his eyes off of Carmen. "She's really pretty, Ry. And she can *sing!*"

He blushes. Tearing his eyes away from the stage, he leans toward me. "I may not be coming back to campus with you later, OK?"

I take a minute to let what my best friend just said settle in. (Is he joking? I take a good look at his face. Nope, I don't think he is.)

"Yeah, sure. I'm cool with that," I say.

But really, I'm not.

MAGGIE

I have seen them perform many times, but the gig tonight at Gallagher's is *el mejor*, the best. Carmen is singing like she is onstage in Vegas—clear and confident and with just the right amount of drama. The guys are playing so good now that they are practicing more often. Ever since the drummer, Lenny, made some CDs and sent them out to recording companies with a schedule of their gigs, the band is taking itself more seriously. But still, everyone looks pretty relaxed, like they are having a good time. No one messes up the lyrics. No one plays too long or forgets a part of their solo (this used to happen a lot). After tonight, I can believe that maybe someday I will hear them on the radio. Who knows? Crazier things have happened.

And speaking of crazy, that cadet is falling hard for Carmen. I sit with Britney and Sara, my two friends from Main Line Vo-Tech, and we are just a few tables back. The shy one, he never takes his eyes off Carmen. Not for a second. And then at the end, when she tells the crowd this will be the last song and it is a new one and it is dedicated to someone in the room who is a special friend—all the men make taunting noises, but not in a bad way, more in an "I wish I was that guy" way. A few of them look around to see if they can tell who Carmen is singing to, but most of them are too drunk now to care.

Meanwhile, the cadet, he is squirming in his seat and his friend is hitting him lightly on the arm as if to say, *It's you, dude!* and then Carmen starts to sing "Red-Faced Boy" and *¡qué chévere!* now I think this new song sounds even better with the whole band and Carmen singing her heart out and playing to the crowd and then the crowd repeating the refrain and then applause and more applause and bows and waves good-bye see you all next time. And that poor cadet looks like he might die right there in his chair—from joy or embarrassment, I can't tell. Or maybe it's because Carmen isn't onstage anymore and he doesn't know where she went and he is desperate to see her again. And I am laughing a little at this boy's innocence, which I think is kind of sweet but maybe not so good for him later on.

Carmen's exit is my cue: I walk over to the cadets and tell the shy one that he should follow me. I open the door just behind the bar that leads to a narrow hall, which leads to a private room for guests of the manager. "In there," I say. "Good luck."

The shy boy looks at me, extends his hand. "I'm Ryan Sweeney."

"Maggie Ruíz," I reply.

"Very nice to meet you, Maggie. Um . . . will I be needing luck?"

I look at his handsome face, his puppy eyes. I feel like those mommies putting their little ones on the bus for the first day of kindergarten, knowing what I know and what he doesn't about my friend.

"Carmen's mother was a Gypsy. Her grandmother is a Gypsy. And for a Gypsy, luck is everything."

He thinks about this for a minute, then nods like he understands. "OK, Maggie. Thanks. Good to know."

I watch him hurry down the hall leading to the room where, at one of the candlelit booths, Carmen is waiting.

CARMEN

Lenny, Nick, and Jorge, they are surprised when I tell them I am meeting someone after the show. They want to go to a place on South Street in the city and celebrate because tonight we had an excellent gig, and Lenny talks to a guy who is here from New York and the guy, he gives Lenny his name and studio address and says send him four copies of our best songs on CD. And is this not exactly what the cards have predicted? Eight of diamonds—*skill is rewarded.*

And now soon I will be alone for the first time with Ryan the shy cadet. And have the cards not also predicted this? Two of hearts—*a romance is possible.* I would be a fool to ignore this boy who inspired our new song that is getting more applause than anything we've ever played before. It's true that I am tired after singing; it's true that I want to celebrate on South Street with my band. But also I am not wanting to be ungrateful, because who knows how long this good luck will last?

"You think the cadet will come tonight?" I ask Maggie when we are at her house before the show and I am finishing my hair and makeup. And Maggie is being a good sister and saying *claro,* of course he is coming. But also she is being an honest friend to remind me of other times when I am flirting with a boy and paying him special attention (boys like Mario, Paul, Evan, Jason, Kurt), and then that boy, he thinks I love him, and then I am just as quick growing tired of him, and then he is getting confused and hurt. Maggie says she knows it is just my nature, that I need my space and my freedom always, that I don't want to be mean. But now these boys are starting to be men and she tells me I should be more careful with them.

"So what are you saying I should do?" I ask her. "I am almost seventeen and now maybe I should go and be a nun?"

Maggie is on the floor studying her flash cards. She holds up her finger to tell me wait while she repeats the names of all the foot bones so she can pass her anatomy test on Monday. So I wait. I am glad when Maggie studies and I think someday she will be a very good animal doctor.

"If you like this boy, you should tell him that your music comes first and that you are always needing *libertad*, your freedom, and if he's OK with that, then you can see him with a clear conscience."

Maggie is right, of course. All the boys I have known, they are always wanting to put a leash around my neck and parade me in front of their friends. *Look—this is my Carmen. . . . Isn't she a pretty little thing?* And all the time they are wanting to see me more and touch me more and they are saying: *Carmen, put down that guitar and pay more attention to* me. And that is when I say: *No more. Good-bye.* ¡Adiós! (In this way, too, I think that maybe I am like my mother.)

So, OK the cards have shown me good things. Mother Mary,

she is hearing my prayers. In return for my good fortune, in return for my blessings, in return for the good show we did tonight, I must be honest with this boy. I must not let him think that he owns my heart. No. No one can own Carmen's heart.

My wrist itches. Footsteps. Ah, yes. Here is my muse—here is the red-faced boy.

RYAN

The room is small and dimly lit. There are three round tables and two booths and Carmen sits at the farthest one, waiting. She smiles when she sees me, and it's like there's a freight train inside my chest. I hope I don't look as nervous as I feel (but I probably do).

"So, Ryan Sweeney from Springfield who is a third-year cadet at VFMA . . . how did you like the show?"

I don't bother to ask how she found out all that. Maybe she looked me up on the Web site, or maybe Will told her, or maybe she's already flirted with half my classmates, I don't know! I push that last thought quickly out of my head.

"I thought you were great. I mean . . . really . . . you were awesome."

Carmen laughs that laugh that makes my stomach do flip-flops. For the past two weeks, ever since I saw her at the Quikmart, it's like there's a recording of it in my head. It's not one of those giggly, twittery laughs that most girls have, but a deep, passionate one, like she means it.

"And the last song . . . ?" I don't finish my question. I'm pretty sure it's self-explanatory.

"Aah, you like?"

"Well, yeah. Sure. I just . . . you know . . . I just wanted to know if it was me you were singing about."

Carmen laughs harder this time, throwing her chin back and shaking her shoulders.

"Well, soldier boy, do you see anyone else back here?" She leans forward and extends her hands, palms up, across the table. I take them and feel something like electricity shoot up my arms. I look straight into those amazing green eyes and think: *If I have a heart attack now, I die a happy man.*

"Joey!" Carmen turns and shouts over her right shoulder. "Two whiskeys!"

Somewhere behind her, I hear glasses sliding across a shelf. Once I left the main room, I realized that the entire back of the building consists of a maze of small rooms and narrow hallways. Suddenly I feel like I'm in one of those Mafia movies—like everyone else knows what's happening and I'm the only clueless one. There must be another room behind ours, but it's too dark for me to see very far. I squint into the corner and glimpse the outline of a small black animal, a cat, I think, which I didn't notice before.

"Yours?" I ask, pointing at whatever's behind the pair of eyes that are staring me down.

"That's Baji. . . . She comes with me when I sing—for good luck."

I laugh. This girl is full of surprises. "Most people travel with their dogs. They're much better company," I offer.

Carmen nods. "*Sí*, I like dogs, too. Very friendly. But they are, you know, so needy . . . so *close*." She makes a face like she has tasted something unpleasant. "Baji, she is not like that. She likes to come and go and that is fine with me. She comes back, OK. She leaves, OK. She is like a tiny tiger—and no one owns a tiger."

I think about my mother's pair of declawed Persians, whose most daring daily adventure consists of moving from the couch to the piano bench. Any tiger-like genes they'd once possessed had been bred out of them long ago. I glance over again at Baji—eyes glaring, white-tipped tail flicking in the corner. I can imagine her having our Persians for breakfast.

Carmen takes my right hand in both of hers and turns it over. With two fingers, she strokes my palms—from wrist to fingertips—several times. She spreads out my fingers. She tilts my hand toward the light.

"You have strong hands, a good life line!" she announces. I'm guessing Maggie was right about her being half Gypsy. In my family, hands are only good for carrying guns or flags. In Carmen's, I guess you carry a map of your future.

"You want me to tell you the rest?" she asks.

"You mean the rest of my, uh, *life*?"

She looks up, her eyes narrowed. Oh God, now she thinks I'm making fun of her.

"You don't believe in fate, Ryan Sweeney?"

"Yeah—I mean, yes, sure, sure I do. . . . Go ahead. Tell me what you see!"

Carmen's not stupid, though. She senses my skepticism, but to my great relief, she ignores it.

"See this here?" she asks, tracing the line that runs diagonally from the base of my index finger to the center of my wrist.

"This means you will have a long life and good health." She moves then to the smaller line that runs across the top of my palm. "And this . . . this means you will travel." Then she frowns, fingering the third line, which lies between the first two. She asks me to close my hand, then open it again. More stroking of the palm. More tilting to the light.

"Is that one bad?" I ask.

She shrugs. "Not good or bad, just *la vida* . . . life."

"Go ahead, tell me. I can take it."

She traces the third line from beginning to end. I shiver. "This means violence. Bloodshed. Someone hurt."

She looks sad all of a sudden. I want to climb across the table and hold her.

"Well, sure. Of course. I'm a military guy, right? I mean, at some point, I suppose I do fight, and I guess someone gets hurt." I take both of her hands in mine and try to reassure her. "I'll just have to make sure it's the other guy. . . ."

The whiskeys arrive, delivered by an old man who disappears as quickly as he enters.

Carmen raises her glass and I meet it with mine. "To music and . . . ?" She hesitates.

"To fate, whatever it brings," I declare. And for once, I say the exact right thing. She smiles and her eyes shine like a pair of giant emeralds.

For the next three hours, we drink and laugh and talk. We each leave once to use the restroom, and in that five minutes or so, it occurs to me that anyone from A Company who saw me here tonight would not believe it. Hell, I can hardly believe it. . . .

Awkward, uptight, never do anything to upset the family or the Academy—that was me, all right. *Before* tonight. I remember the one time my father caught me and Will drinking vodka in the woods with one of the older neighbor kids. He dragged me into the garage and let me have it across the back of the legs with his belt. I couldn't sit for a week. I raise my glass and think: *This is for you, Colonel Sweeney!* and drink my fill.

At two a.m., the bar shuts down and Joey reappears, waving a set of car keys, saying he will take me wherever I need to go. Carmen walks me out the back door. But before I get into the car, she reaches up, wraps her arms around my neck, and kisses me.

Part 3

There's a cure for every ill when you

have a Gypsy for a sweetheart.

❧ *Prosper Mérimée, CARMEN*

WILL

So I'm tossing and turning in the dark, wondering if Ryan ran into trouble with the townies, or if he went home with Carmen, or if . . . ?

I try calling him twice, but he's not answering. My bedside clock reads 2:30. Damn. Why am I losing sleep over this? I mean, I've been waiting years for Ryan to break a rule, to loosen up and have some fun for once. But this is like . . . I don't know . . . *sudden*. Maybe I should try to sneak back out and find him.

I decide to wait. Another ten minutes pass. At 2:40, a wedge of light spills into the room. The door closes quickly.

"Christ, Ry, I was starting to think you'd gone AWOL!"

"Oh, good. . . . You're awake."

"Damn right I'm awake. I was just lying here wondering if I should come find you—and if I *couldn't* find you, what I'd say to the four hundred guys who just might notice your empty seat at first mess." I prop myself up on my elbow, curious to see what shape my roommate's in after his first-ever night on the town. "Is that whiskey I smell . . . ?"

Ryan turns on the small desk lamp, then quickly bends the metal neck so the light won't be seen by anyone outside. He rummages around in his drawer, pulls out a bottle of mouthwash, and sets it on his desk. "For the morning," he explains. He flicks off the light, slips off his shoes, and stretches out on his bed.

"So, you gonna tell me what happened?" I ask.

Ryan exhales loudly. I wait.

"Don't know if I can. I mean—yeah, OK, I'll answer any question you ask, but I'm not sure I can explain in words what happened to me tonight."

"Did you get lucky?"

Ryan laughs, then slaps his hand over his mouth; the dorm walls are thin and there's always someone patrolling. "No—not in the way you mean." He turns to face me. "C'mon, Will. Give me a *little* credit. I'm a guy, but I'm no predator."

"Well, you could've fooled me the way you were locked onto her the whole night. I honestly think the place could've burned down around us and you wouldn't have even noticed."

"Was it *that* obvious?"

"Yeah, it was," I reply. (Like I said, though—Ryan is a hard guy to be *mad* at.) "She *is* hot, Ry," I add. "I'm not questioning your taste." Ryan is silent for a moment.

"Well, after tonight, I'm questioning everything," he says finally. "Why I'm here, who I am, what my future is . . . everything. With Carmen, I feel like a totally changed person. She's so different from anyone I've ever met."

I think about the girls who come to our dances and to our other social events at the Academy. They're all from private schools and good families, well dressed and well behaved.

The word "tame" comes to mind. Next to them, Carmen seems almost exotic.

A little dangerous.

"I'm in love with her, Will. . . ."

I take a minute to digest this information. I wait to see if Ryan explains or qualifies it. He doesn't.

"Ry . . . I have to say, I'm happy for you. After seventeen years of living as a model citizen, it's about time you had some fun in your life. And it's good that you're starting to question some things. But hey, man, you just met this chick—"

"*Carmen!*" Ry corrects me in a voice that's way too loud for these walls and this hour. He gets a grip, though, and continues in an agitated whisper. "Her name's *Carmen* and she's not some 'chick' and I *love* her, OK?"

I fall back on my pillow. I stare at the ceiling and wonder if the pressure of being Cadet Captain Ryan Sweeney, son of Colonel Michael Sweeney, brother of U.S. Army Captain Adam Sweeney— on his second tour of duty in Iraq—has finally made him crack.

MAGGIE

I wait in the car with my brother who says OK he will drive us to work today, but Carmen is not coming out of the house. I know she stayed very late at the pub with that boy Ryan Sweeney, and I am betting you six movie tickets and dessert at Dairy Queen that she is still asleep. I ring her cell phone but no one answers.

"*Espérate*. Wait here," I tell Marco. I run around to the back door and let myself in. No sign of her *abuelos*—probably they got a ride to church. I go up the stairs two at a time and bang on her bedroom door. "Hey! Sleeping Beauty . . . Carmen . . . come on, *¡apúrate!* Hurry up or Fat Frank will fire us for sure!"

Faster than I can make a foot-long sandwich, we are both in Marco's Honda and flying down Route 202. Carmen changes into her work clothes in the backseat, and I am pinching Marco hard on the arm every time he tries to sneak a look in the rearview mirror. I hand her my brush and a ponytail holder and one of my cereal bars. "Sometimes I am such a *tonta*. A fool! What would I do without my Maggie, *mi hermana*, my angel sister," she says, and leans forward to kiss me on the cheek. I laugh at this remark because yes, OK, Carmen is exhausted—but she is nobody's fool.

Marco leaves us at the corner and we walk together the half

block to the store. Carmen is thanking me again and again because we are on time for work even though she was sleeping only twenty minutes ago, and until she makes it big in the music business, she needs her job at the Quikmart.

All morning we are just working, working, working because there is a soccer tournament down the street and all those soccer mommies and daddies and their kids with muddy shoes and numbers on their backs are coming in for drinks and snacks and sandwiches. At one-forty-five, Vicky with the purple hair and too many piercings comes in for her shift. I ask Frank if maybe Carmen and me can have a break and he scratches his pregnant belly and says OK but to be quick about it and be sure to pay for any food we eat. I look at the ring on his left hand and I wonder what sort of desperate woman would marry him.

We go out back and lean against the sunny side of the building. Carmen drinks a Diet Coke and has a cigarette and that's how I know she's so tired, because she says smoking is bad for her voice. I drink a Gatorade and eat a tuna fish sandwich and let the sun warm my face.

"So your new boy . . . ?" I ask between bites. "Ryan . . . is he really so shy?"

Carmen grins and takes a long drag from her Marlboro Light. She exhales slowly so that one small cloud of smoke hangs in front of us like a friendly ghost.

"*Sí*, he is *bien tímido*. Really shy. And he likes me. He likes my songs."

I wait for her to go on, but she stops talking. I finish my drink and toss the bottle into the recycle bin. "And of course, you are telling this shy Ryan who likes you and your songs that you are first in love with your dream of becoming a rich and famous singer who drives all over the country in a tour bus and whose voice we hear every day on the radio." I pause, so I am sure Carmen is hearing me. "And of course you are also telling him that he should not get too sure of your affection because of this, right?"

And Carmen, she is looking guilty like Marco and Carlos do when they come in smelling like beer and laughing down the hallway late at night, and my mother, she is waiting for them in the kitchen to tell them they will come with her to confession tomorrow and *¡ay Dios mío!* why is she spending her life scrubbing toilets if they are going to be crazy good-for-nothing sons? But I don't want Carmen to feel guilty . . . no. I just want her to be honest with this boy because you can see it is just a game for her but for him it is no game.

"No, Maggie. I didn't tell him this. Not exactly. But I will." Carmen faces me and makes the sign of the cross on her chest. "I promise I will do this very soon."

We rest our tired shoulders against the building. The back door opens a crack. "Hey, you two, break's over. We got customers . . . ," Fat Frank yells out to us.

Carmen takes a final drag from her cigarette, then blows out the smoke in short little puffs. One of them looks exactly like a heart, and we laugh and point as it drifts over the hedge and disappears into the wind.

WILL

It took me five minutes of hard shaking, some shouting, and finally, a cup of water to get Ryan out of bed. Once on his feet, I have to admit, he looked awful—and I don't have to tell you that dark glasses are not part of the uniform here at Valley Forge. He did the best he could with a cold shower and half a bottle of mouthwash, but that only went so far.

Now, as he marches in the bright Sunday sun beside the sober, well-rested guys in A Company, he still looks only half alive.

"Captain Sweeney, present your company!" Colonel Frasier barks from his position on the hill. The colonel is second in command here, and he takes his job very seriously.

Somehow, Ryan gets everyone through the preinspection drill and into formation for the colonel. As we pass in our separate lines, he shoots me a desperate look. His face is green; I try not to imagine what will happen if the contents of his stomach end up on the colonel's boots.

"A Company. Halt. Pres*ennnt!*" Ryan shouts in a voice that's far less commanding than usual. I glance quickly along the rows of eyes in A Company, relieved that they haven't yet noticed anything out of the ordinary. But even from where I'm standing—a row behind and a few guys down—I can see that Ryan's collar isn't straight, that his pants aren't creased, and that his shoes need to be shined.

With the morning sun glinting off his medals, Colonel Frasier begins his inspection in the lower ranks, then works his way past those of us in the middle and farther up the line. Except for an occasional nervous twitch of his chin, his face remains stoic, his expression unchanged. As he approaches Ryan, I feel my own pulse quicken. With most of the other officers, including General Hirshman, watching us from the perimeter, I can't break formation or even turn my head. Instead, I try to shift my eyes so that whatever happens to Ryan will fall into the scope of my peripheral vision.

Colonel Frasier stops and squares himself in front of my roommate. He studies Ryan's face, then his jacket, pants, sword, and shoes. He leans in and whispers something in Ryan's ear, then strides purposefully back to the middle of the parade grounds, where he salutes the general and takes his place beside the other officers.

Sergeant O'Connor takes over now, marching us through our formations and honing every drill. As we spin and twirl, double-step, pivot, and reverse, the sergeant's voice becomes more urgent, and it strikes me for the first time how much he sounds like Ryan's father.

When I pass Ryan for the second time, he's still pretty green, his sword held straight up before his face, his middle finger twitching.

RYAN

At morning inspection and parade, Colonel Frasier whispers an invitation for me to "have a little chat" with him in his office. I report directly. He keeps it brief:

CF: Captain Sweeney, I broke one of my personal rules today. . . . I made an exception for you . . . and I *never* make exceptions!!

ME: Yes sir.

CF: Up until today, you've been a model student, a model cadet, a model human being—and what's more, I know the general has high hopes that you'll go on to West Point and show them what kind of men we produce here at VFMA.

ME: Yes sir.

CF: I don't know why today, of all days, Captain Sweeney, you chose to not prepare for inspection, why your eyes are redder than my wife's nail polish and your breath smells faintly of whiskey. . . .

ME: Yes sir. I mean no sir. I mean—

CF: Shut up, Sweeney!

ME: Yes sir.

CF [*pacing in front of his desk, pulling at his medals and muttering*

words I can't make out, then returning to face me]: If you think for one minute that I'm not watching you . . . if you think for one *second* that I'll let you off the hook again . . . then listen up: NO MORE EXCEPTIONS! . . . You got that, Sweeney?
ME: Yes sir.
CF [*saluting crisply*]: Dismissed.

At the halfway point of our "chat," I consider trying to explain. But then—really—what *could* I say that he'd believe or forgive? Nothing. There is nothing I can say, nothing I can do but wait for him to finish. When he does, I salute, turn, and leave the office.

Outside, I walk quickly around the next building and dash behind the gym, where I am so violently ill I half expect to look down and find my stomach on the ground.

When I've recovered enough to walk again, I head back to the dorm. I lie on my bed, close my eyes, and think of Carmen—her face, her hands, her hair, her voice—and drift off to sleep.

MAGGIE

This week at Main Line Vo-Tech, we are studying the circulatory system—the blood and where it goes and how it goes and what it is made of—and *buzz buzz buzz* there goes my phone and now I have to look: **deliv @ 5 come over.** I am on the bus and trying to read over my biology notes that I scribbled down today in class before the teacher said that's all, quiz on Thursday, good-bye.

But after this phone message, *¡ay bendito!* it's no use. The whole way home my eyes are pointed down at my list of blood words—"platelet," "capillary," "vein"—but my mind is guessing what this delivery is and worrying that maybe Carmen has started to get careless about her deals with Will the blond cadet and maybe now they are doing their cigarette business at home. But then I am reminding myself that Carmen, she is much too smart for this. And I am thinking maybe this delivery is about her music and perhaps it is a new guitar. Yes, that could be it. A new guitar. But Carmen is very superstitious and she treats her old guitar (she has played it since she was nine years old) like a baby, and no, she would have told me if she is getting a new one.

I get off at the corner, and already I can see the big white delivery truck in front of Carmen's house. I walk fast and soon I see her *abuelos* standing on the porch, both of them old and frail with backs that are bent at the same angle from so many years on this earth. Sometimes I can hardly tell them apart, and they remind me of those matched sets of salt and pepper shakers I have seen at the flea market.

"*Maggeeeee!*" Carmen yells, and waves when she sees me hurrying. I join them on the porch, and we wait to see what is coming out of the truck with two big men who are opening the back and securing the wooden ramp. Carmen's grandmother starts to get upset, and she speaks very fast and wrings her hands. Carmen, she is trying to explain to her grandmother how it is OK that these men are here, and yes, they are bringing something Carmen has paid for, and no, they are not coming into the house for any bad reason or to take anything away.

And now down the wooden ramp is coming a rocking chair wrapped in heavy plastic, and it waits on the sidewalk while the men go back in to get the matching recliner. Then one at a time these new things are being lifted inside by the two men from the furniture store and then the rip, rip, ripping of the plastic from the beautiful chairs and then yellow and white forms, sign here, please, miss, and Carmen signs and then thank you, good-bye to the two men and their truck.

We stand all four of us in the living room, waiting. Finally: "You buy these things, Carmencita? For us?" Señor Navarro asks in the quiet voice of a kind old man.

"*Sí, Abuelito.* They are for you—for your anniversary. For your fifty years together. Come on . . . let's see how they fit you. . . . Come on, Abuelita, you two . . . sit down!"

And now the two old people Carmen loves even more than her music, now they are both touching these chairs and shaking their heads like they are in a dream. Carmen and me, we are helping them, and see, you pull like this and the chair comes up under your legs, and the *abuelos* are giggling and crying for joy at the same time. We are this way for a while in that living room, and Carmen and me, we are laughing at these two in their new chairs and we are having a little Christmastime in April.

After a while, we go outside to sit on the porch steps and leave the *abuelos* to watch their shows on TV. Baji appears instantly from someplace she's been hiding and brushes against my ankle.

"You are buying those chairs with your money from smuggling the cigarettes?" I ask Carmen, drawing the cat onto my lap and removing two ticks from her smooth black coat.

"*Sí*, mostly . . . and some from just my paycheck."

I pretend to search Baji for more bugs, but really I am thinking how I feel about this. Not so much about the smuggling cigarettes, because Carmen and me, we have already had that talk. But this money . . . this money that Mike the driver is using for his sick wife and that Carmen could be using for other things.

"You are not wanting to save some of this money for your future—in case you want to go back to school?"

Carmen looks past me down the street to where a few of the neighborhood kids are playing kickball while their young mothers, a few with babies on their hips, are watching.

"Maggie, *mi hermana*," she says, and puts her arm around my shoulders, "you are always trying, eh? You are always looking out for me." She sighs and keeps her eyes on the kids and their game. "It is you who must be the smart one with the books. It is you who must go to college and become a good animal doctor. It is a good and happy life. And you will do this, I know it."

And whenever Carmen says these things, I believe her. I believe her because whatever Carmen predicts about someone's future is usually coming true. Like the time I ask about my brother Carlos, who is sweet until he is drinking and then he is crazy and rages like a bull. Carmen reads the cards and tells me there will be trouble for him soon. And do you know just four days later my brother is arrested for driving drunk and fighting? And like the time I ask her what should I do: stay in school or go to work full-time to help Mami with the bills? Carmen reads the cards and says a woman not in my family will lead me to a good place and *boom*, just like that, the next week I am talking with the counselor at school and I am signing up for my first classes at Vo-Tech and everyone there says Maggie, you keep up your good grades and we will find you scholarships for college.

Suddenly Baji has had enough of me. She squirms free and gives me a little bite on my arm as she leaves. Carmen and me, we sit on the steps and talk awhile and watch the kids play in the street. I wipe the red place on my arm and tell her about my classes and how the blood in one human body travels more than sixty thousand miles and why on the legs of old people you can see the veins like highway maps but not on ours, *gracias a Dios*. Carmen tells me how she is praying every night to Mother Mary that the man from the studio in New York is liking their new CD and will ask them to sign a contract. She tells me she thinks Ryan the shy cadet is very cute and that she is meeting him at Valley Forge Park this weekend. But also she is not wanting to see him too often because she needs more time to write songs in case the man from New York calls and says Carmen, I will make you a star.

CARMEN

Just because I dropped out of high school, just because I work at the Quikmart and wear clothes from the discount stores . . . this doesn't mean I don't think about the way things are and how someday maybe I can change them. *Mis abuelos,* they come here on the boat from Spain when they are young. They marry and settle down and they don't make trouble. They work hard their whole lives and who takes care of them? No one. My grandfather all his life in the sheet-metal factory. My grandmother for fifty years washing and mending and sewing people's nice clothes. Their only daughter, my mother, they don't know where she is, and she is never coming back, that's for sure. Abuelita has told me that even as a child my mother was too wild for them—they could do nothing to keep her from trouble. Abuelita says she could read it in the cards and she could read it in the tea leaves and even on the palm of my mother's beautiful hand. Abuelita says she knew what must come to pass, but she did not want to believe it. Then my mother, she leaves home at age seventeen and is lost to them for three years. One day she comes back with a little girl screaming on her hip. They know then what has happened and they know, too, that this is the last time they will see their daughter, and even though it breaks their hearts, they say *adiós* to that wild one.

So I try not to make trouble for them. I try not to worry them. I try to buy them nice things once in a while and take them to the free medical clinic and to the grocery store and to church. I think maybe God gave me this voice so I can use it to make a better life for them and for me, too. I know *mi abuela* prays hard for me when the boys come around. I know *mi abuelo* shakes his head and crosses his heart when I leave for a gig in a tight skirt and high heels. I know they are remembering my mother and they are thinking I will end up the same. But they are wrong. My spirit is wild, yes—but I am no fool. I love the boys but I will not belong to any one of them. I am free. Always free. And if I leave, it will be because my voice has given us a chance to have a better life. Yes—a better life. No more food stamps for *mis abuelos*. And no more getting turned away at the doctor's because they can't afford to pay. No more weekend shifts behind the counter with Fat Frank's bad breath and a paycheck that is never enough.

Tonight, after Maggie leaves and my grandparents are asleep in their new chairs, I go down to the Cave. I light the candles and put food out for Baji, who is good luck. I spread the cards all around me. The Fates guide my hand—one card, two cards, three cards. I push the others away. I turn my chosen cards over one at a time: the two of hearts *(¡ay, otra vez!)* . . . a romance is building; the jack of hearts—ah . . . a determined young man. (Ha, yes, I have already met this one.) My fate is heavily red, heavily tilted toward affairs of the heart. Now the third card: the nine of spades. This means worries and conflicts lie ahead. *(¡Ay Señor!)*

I sit with Baji on my lap and stare at the three cards before me. Abuelita says the cards never lie and I believe her. She also says that God and Jesus and Mother Mary watch over us all the time and we should pray to them for the strength to face our fortunes—good or bad. I believe that, too. So now I pray for strength to face whatever lies ahead. Yes. Whatever lies ahead.

April 3, 2007

Dear Ryan:

Today when I saw that the last bit of ice had melted on the reservoir, I remembered how you and Will loved to go fishing there almost every Saturday. Your father would have his hands full trying to find you and drag you both home before dark! I'm sure your weekends are slightly busier now . . . but I hope you're still finding a little time to relax and think of us.

Not much is new around here. Now that he's officially retired from active duty, the Colonel keeps himself busy traveling, lecturing, and recruiting on behalf of Uncle Sam. On weekends, he wages war against the vines and underbrush that took over the yard last year (yes, I do realize it's only April, but he's getting an early start!).

As you well know, your father isn't one to gush compliments or write letters. But even so, I want you to realize, Ryan, honey, that we are both so very proud of your excellent grades and your being captain of your company. I hope you don't mind, but I have been bragging to everyone in my garden club. They all ask about you when we have our monthly lunch meetings— especially Luanne Gudel, Lauren's mom. Do you ever hear from Lauren? It'll be wonderful when you're home for the summer and you two can spend some time together.

I hope you are taking good care of yourself and I

hope Will is, too. *Tell him we said hello. I haven't always liked the idea of your living at the Academy and having to miss out on family life. But knowing that Will's there with you has made that more bearable, somehow.*

Well, I'd better go—your father will be home soon. Study hard, honey. Eat right and get enough sleep. And remember how much we love you and how proud you've made us.

Love and kisses,
Mom

RYAN

True to his word, Colonel Frasier didn't report me for my poor showing at Sunday's inspection and parade, but he *did* make sure I was assigned to extra duties. So tonight, while the rest of A Company attends the wrestling match against Haverford Prep, I'm standing guard at the front gate with Kyle Vanderkamp and David Long. Kyle's a second classman (that's what they call juniors here) like me, the right guard on the football team, and kind of a hothead. He hasn't said, but my guess is he's out here tonight because of some fight he picked with one of the other players. David's a shy kid, complete with freckles and wire-rimmed glasses, a harmless, obedient fourth classman (freshman) from Virginia.

Front-gate duty is the worst. It's the only perimeter post where you're constantly exposed and there's no chance to rest or take a whiz behind a bush or do anything but march back and forth like you're some target in one of those shooting-gallery video games. Most of the time, you pray for a vehicle to come through, just so you have something to do.

At least tonight the weather's good; almost perfect, in fact: warm and dry, with an evening breeze that smells like cherry blossoms. The wild rosebushes that line the inside of the wall are starting to bloom, and one of them is blood-red, like the flower Carmen gave me . . . like my face (I guess) when she handed me that rose . . . like the blouse she wore when she sang on Saturday . . . like her lips when she kissed me before I had to leave that night. Carmen. I'm not sure if I can make it from weekend to weekend without seeing her. This afternoon, I sent her a message: **r u free anytime sat?** And she sent me one back: **for u i will be free after 3.**

"Sweeney!" Vanderkamp hisses from about twenty yards away, startling me from what was turning into a really fine daydream. I realize I've completely missed my turnaround, so he must think I'm leaving my post and heading to the dorms.

"Sorry, Kamp," I say once I've corrected my course and we're marching within a few yards of each other. "I thought I saw something moving over by the edge of the parade grounds . . . but it wasn't anything after all." Part of me is shocked at how quickly I'm becoming a liar. But then again, I've never been in love before. And doesn't everyone say that love makes you do a lot of strange things—stuff you thought you would never do? My newfound talent for bending the truth proves that, I guess.

"Probably that stray cat," Kamp says as we pass the next time through our paces.

"What?" I ask.

"The last two nights I had duty out here, there's been this black cat hanging around the street by the gate. It usually sits right about there." He points to the brick pillar from which the entry gate swings like a huge iron wing. "The first night it was quiet, but the second night it howled and meowed and wouldn't shut up for anything. Gave me the creeps, it did. I don't walk under ladders,

I don't travel on Friday the thirteenth—and I *really* don't like black cats!"

I chuckle at the image of superstitious Vanderkamp strutting back and forth with his rifle, being serenaded by a friendly feline. "She probably just wanted to be pals with you, Kamp," I say sarcastically. "You know you *are* the sociable type. . . ."

Vanderkamp frowns, but since I outrank him, he shrugs it off.

"Hey, speak of the devil!" Kamp says, pointing the butt of his rifle toward the gate.

And then I see it, too: a small black cat with one white paw and a waving white-tipped tail. I blink once, twice. Still there. The animal appeared so fast, as if out of thin air. It's Baji, all right, her green eyes gleaming in the full-moon evening like a pair of polished emeralds. She sits down next to the gate and looks straight at me, her tail flicking back and forth along the ground.

Suddenly something small and flat skids just off her left side. I turn in time to see Kamp reaching for another stone from the gravel beds along the inside of the wall.

I don't remember much after this. I know I leap for him with a swiftness that amazes even me. I know I hit him with my fist at least twice, catching him once square in the chin. I know he pummels my head, my neck, and my arms until they feel like stone and I pass out on the grass.

When I finally wake up, someone's holding my head. David Long is staring at me wide-eyed through his glasses, his lips quivering. Kamp is being restrained by two of the older guys from A Company. I turn my head toward the gate. Baji sits at the foot of the brick pillar, cleaning her one white foot. I blink, and she's gone.

MAGGIE

Today while I am in anatomy lab, Carmen leaves a phone message: Take the bus to Lenny's house and you can study while we rehearse and then Lenny will drive us both to work the evening shift. Lenny the drummer's garage sits apart from his house in the backyard and for now this is where the Gypsy Lovers are having their rehearsals. Inside, the air is thick with the smell of old tires and motor oil, but Lenny, he says the doors must stay closed when they play so the neighbors don't complain.

Lenny has thrown a blanket over a big wooden box filled with rusty car parts and wires and God knows what, and tonight this is my study table. I put my cell phone on the workbench close by and also Carmen's phone in case her *abuela* calls. At first, I try not to listen to the band so I can read the chapter and review the pictures in my text: *Digestive Systems of Some Common Animals*. But then after a while, I think it is not so bad to have this music playing as I am reading about the esophagus of the horse (it doesn't move in reverse, so a horse can't throw up) and the stomachs of cows (they have four!) and trying to memorize the chart with all the glands and what slimy substance each of them secretes.

At six o'clock, I take a break from liver, pancreas, and bile.

I stand up, stretch, and watch them rehearsing a song that Lenny has written.

"Can we skip the second refrain? It's too long there," Carmen says when they are done playing it once.

"I think we could back off on the bass after the first verse," Jorge suggests, adjusting his strings. "Bring it in again stronger at the end."

"OK. That's cool. I can move the drum solo to just after the third verse, too," Lenny adds.

After this, there is more singing and playing and stopping. More talking about what to change and what sounds good and then OK, let's try it again. When I watch them in this oil-stained corner of Lenny's garage, breathing air that stings your lungs but singing like they are on a big stage in Atlantic City, this makes me think maybe rehearsing is just as hard as studying. Maybe harder. Because who knows if all these hours of practice and let's try it again will someday be money in their pockets?

Something is buzzing. *¡Coño!* It's Carmen's phone. But this is not her *abuelo*'s number.

"Hello?"

Nobody there. Then: "Hello . . . uh . . . is Carmen there?"

Ah, the shy Ryan. "She's busy," I tell him. "Can you call back?"

"Is this Maggie?"

"Uh-huh . . . and I am busy, too, so—"

"What's she doing?" he interrupts.

Now, maybe I don't know much about boys, but right away I am thinking, *That is none of your business, shy Ryan.* But of course, I am polite and do not say this.

"She's working. Rehearsing. You have to call her back."

"You can't interrupt her—for just a minute?"

Ha! This boy does not know Carmen.

"No. I can't."

Silence. Then: "OK, well—tell her that I called and that I'll meet her Saturday at the park, like we planned."

"Yeah. OK. I will tell her . . . at the park."

He's still on the phone, I can tell. The band has stopped playing and they are taking a water break.

"Hey, Maggie?"

Ay bendito, this boy is stubborn like a donkey. "*¿Qué? What?*"

"Does Carmen, you know—uh—does she see anyone else? I mean—she's not, you know, *involved* with anyone . . . is she?"

I glance over to the band. Lenny is sharing a large Aquafina with Carmen, and they are talking and pointing to their music. I know Lenny has liked Carmen for a while, but Carmen says with the band she must be all business or it will ruin everything.

"No. Carmen is not steady with another guy, if that is what you mean," I tell him, even though I think he is still being too pushy. But maybe now he will leave me alone. "I will give her your message. I have to go now." I push END. I close the phone. I find my place on the page and read the rest of the chapter as the band begins to play again and Carmen's voice fills up the oily garage: "Let me see you smile, let me take your hand, don't be afraid . . . no, no! You are my darling red-faced boy."

Part 4

Do you know, my friend, I think I love you a little.

But it can't last; dog and wolf don't stay friends for long.

✿ *Prosper Mérimée, CARMEN*

RYAN

General Hirshman canceled all leave requests until noon so he could show us off to a visiting officer. As a result, we spend almost all of Saturday morning on the parade grounds doing drills under the watchful eye of this bigwig British guy, who nods approvingly and twists his goatee as we pass by.

By eleven o'clock, it's above seventy-five degrees, and most of us are in a rolling sweat. As soon as we're dismissed, we disperse like pellets from a shotgun. Will and I double-time it back to the dorms with everyone else. We throw off our uniforms and grab a snack, some water, and my phone. While Will scares up a basketball from somewhere down the hall, I text Carmen: **meet u main gate vf park @ 3, k?**

I don't expect a quick reply. At Gallagher's, she told me she hates cell phones, that she only carries one in case her grandparents need her. "Why should I have to pay so much money to talk to people I see every day?" she explained. "It's annoying . . . like a little boy always following you around and you can never send him home!" I told her that most of the girls I knew spent hours a day on their phones, that they couldn't live without them. "Well, good for them." Carmen shrugged. "I can think of a million better ways to use my time."

Slipping on shorts and sneakers, I think back to some of the other things I learned about her that night: (1) she lives with her elderly grandparents; (2) she dropped out of high school last year, on her sixteenth birthday; (3) she wants to be a professional singer; (4) Maggie Ruíz is, and has always been, her best friend; and (5) except for Philadelphia and one week at the Jersey Shore, she's never traveled anywhere.

Will appears in the doorway, holding up a basketball swiped from some unsuspecting freshman. "Ready to get your ass whipped?" he asks. We bolt out the back door and spend the next hour playing one-on-one half-court and H-O-R-S-E behind the dorm.

"*E*, you soft-bellied suburbanite!" Will roars triumphantly as I miss my fifth shot and he makes his: a nothing-but-net three-pointer from the left side. We slap palms at the top of the key before heading to our water bottles under the trees. Walking off, I realize that this is the first hour since I met her that I've not been constantly thinking about Carmen. For a short time there, it felt like the old days back home—just me and Will, a basketball, and a driveway.

But now it's past one o'clock and I haven't gotten a message back. I feel a small panic rising inside me. What if she forgot? (She couldn't forget, could she? I mean, that kiss . . .) What if Maggie didn't tell her I called? What if she told her the wrong day?

I sip nervously from the water bottle and triple-check my voice mail. Nothing.

"Ready to go again?" Will asks, tossing down his empty bottle and snapping me back to reality.

"Uh . . . sure. Yeah. I can play another twenty minutes, but then I gotta get cleaned up."

Will picks up the ball with his feet and juggles it like a soccer ball. "You meeting that ch— I mean . . . *Carmen* again?"

I'm not sure if Will is jealous of the fact that I have a girlfriend—who happens to be his latest contraband contact— or if he just finds it inconvenient. Either way, I think I was pretty clear when I told him I love her. So why he's surprised I'm seeing her again is, well . . . *surprising*. I'm not in the mood to argue about it, though.

"Yeah. But not till three," I reply, trying to downplay it, even though I know I won't be able to concentrate until she calls or texts me back.

I set the phone on the ground at the edge of the court. We start playing one-on-one again, but this time I'm not into it. Every five minutes or so, I call time-out, run over to the sideline, and check my phone. Finally, Will gets pissed.

"C'mon, Ry. My mom could play better than that. Are you in or out?"

I shrug, check my phone again.

"Fine. Suit yourself." He throws the basketball to the far end of the court, grabs his water bottle, and runs off toward the gym. *He'll get over it*, I tell myself. We've had our minor disagreements before, and he always does.

I stroll aimlessly around the end court, retrieve the ball, take a few halfhearted shots, miss them all. The mid-April sun is intense. I wander back to the shade, take another long drink from my bottle, and finish off a PowerBar. A lone raven, perched on a branch, watches me with unusual interest. I stand up and wave my arms. *Shoooo!*

I watch it fly off. I can't help wondering if it's the same one that stole my lunch that day in the park. The phone vibrates in my hand: **k. see u there @ 3.** I feel the color rise in my face, my heart begin to race. What has this girl done to me?

MAGGIE

Twice already today I have sliced my hand with the bread knife, and all because last night my brothers come in late and one at a time from their beer and girlfriends, and they are like big, clumsy elephants on the stairs and in the hall. I get maybe five hours' sleep. My mother in the morning, she is telling me, "Maggie, if you have sons, you make them leave as soon as they have hair on their faces or you will have nothing but heartache, nothing but trouble!" and I say, "OK, Mami." I give her a big hug and kiss her on the nose because I know she loves her boys, and even though they drive her crazy with worry, she will be sad if they ever *do* leave.

So now I tell my hands that always smell like ham and cheese and mustard to wake up and pay attention so I don't go home with three Band-Aids and a warning from Fat Frank. I am being very careful with my roll-slicing when I get a feeling that someone is watching me. "Hey, Lenny, *¿qué pasa?*"

"Hey, Maggie. Sorry—you looked like you were concentrating there. I didn't want to interrupt you."

And see . . . this is what I like about Lenny, who is handsome and athletic and was once the best high school quarterback in

Philadelphia, but now is just a very good drummer and also
manager for the Gypsy Lovers: he is first thinking about everybody else. Guys like Lenny you half expect to be stuck-up and rude,
which he is not.

"These rolls can wait—you want to order something? We
have a turkey club on a kaiser roll, special today for $3.99. . . ."

"Thanks, sounds good, but I'm not really hungry. . . . I was
hoping to catch Carmen. Is she here?"

"No. She worked till the lunch shift was over. Then she left . . .
to meet a friend." (Should I tell Lenny about the cadet? Would he
care? No, it is Carmen's business only—she can tell Lenny if
she wants. . . .) "You can call her cell phone, though, if it's
important."

Lenny laughs. "She hates that phone! She only has it on about
half the time anyway. That's OK. . . . I'll just wait till I see her so I
can tell her myself."

"You have news?" I say before I can stop myself. I cringe. This
is something I am working on very hard now. I am trying hard not
to be like the girls my age who are always filling their brain with
other people's business, other people's news. I knew when I
started my classes at Vo-Tech that I am no genius, but I am what
you call a worker. And because I probably have only so much
space in my brain, I promised myself I would not be filling it up
with gossip and "Did you hear?" type things. No. I decided I
would fill it with bigger things, things that matter—like the circulatory system and the structure of cells and photosynthesis. And
only once in a while can I let myself look inside a *People* magazine

and read about face-lifts and movie stars and who is cheating on who.

"You don't have to tell—" I begin, but it is too late now.

"That guy from New York," Lenny says, "the one who came to Gallagher's . . . he wants some photos of the band. We have to get everybody together this week at my place and get those done." Lenny is shifting around a little in his boots, maybe deciding if he wants to tell me the rest. He moves closer to the counter and whispers: "He's coming to hear us again in a few weeks—and he's *bringing his boss!*"

And there it is: someone else's business that is none of my business, but now it *is* my business, and I am smiling a little on the outside and very big inside because it is sounding like maybe something good might happen for the Gypsy Lovers and for Carmen.

When I am sure that Fat Frank isn't looking, I hand Lenny an already-made turkey club with mayo on the side.

"No charge, on the house," I tell him.

After Lenny leaves, I slice more rolls and wonder if this is really such a good thing after all for Carmen. I mean, what if the guy comes down with his boss and the band is not playing so good? Or—what if they *do* play good, and the boss man from the studio, he doesn't like their music? What if these New York guys make promises to Carmen and to the Gypsy Lovers, but then . . . nothing happens? No contract, no recording session. No phone calls. Nothing. I hear my mother's voice in my head: *Maggie, you see these hands? You stay in school, you study the books, you have a nice life with money in your pocket.* "OK, Mami," I say to the hoagie roll I am slicing. "OK."

Someone knocking at the back door. *¡Ay bendito!* I am almost forgetting . . .

I promised Carmen I would do her business with Mike the driver. I put down the knife and rolls and slip off my plastic gloves. I open the back door and here is Mike already unloading the boxes of cigarettes from the back of the truck. I grab the clipboard, count the boxes, and sign the forms. I make sure that Fat Frank is still inside before I open the small storage room where we keep the extra trash bags, brooms, squeegees, and other outside cleaning supplies. "Put the last one in there," I tell Mike.

I close the door but do not lock it. The blond cadet, Carmen said, will be coming by later to pick it up.

RYAN

— ❦ —

Since I seem to have pissed off Will, I'll have to find someone else to sign out with me. I grab Jimmy Nolan and Luke Westbrooke, a couple of fourth classmen from Colorado, and tell them they'll be accompanying me on the shuttle to the King of Prussia Mall. They're innocent but not stupid, so they don't protest. They know this is an easy way to win points with me.

"We just walkin' around, or seein' a movie . . . or what, sir?" Jimmy Nolan asks once we're seated in the back of the shuttle.

I shrug. "That's up to you guys. . . . I have a date, so I'll be parting ways with you at the mall." Jimmy and Luke look at me with wide eyes, trying to decide if I'm telling the truth. "But I know that if anyone on campus asks, you guys will say the three of us had a swell time at the mall, just walking around, drinking coffee, hanging out at the bookstore . . . *capiche?*"

Jimmy and Luke nod vigorously. I hand Luke a twenty, just to be sure. "Milk money," I say. "I'll meet you both back at the stop at six."

I watch the two of them head through the mall entrance before I board the shuttle to Valley Forge Park. Seven minutes later, it drops me at the entrance gate, where Carmen is already waiting, dressed in jean shorts and a loose-fitting white blouse, looking like something the gods dropped down from heaven. I flip open my phone and snap a photo. She frowns, then laughs. My heart leaps.

CARMEN

⁓ ⟢ ⁓

"You know, Red." (He blushes when I call him this.) "You shouldn't
think I am stupid just because I dropped out of high school." We
are walking along the trails of the park for almost an hour, and
Ryan is showing off what he knows about the history of what happened here. He is telling me about those officers—Washington,
Lafayette, von Steuben—and about all those men who braved the
hunger and sickness, and how they formed groups and built their
huts from trees and mud (with bare hands and no shoes!) and by
February only half of them were still alive.

I listen because I have always liked this story about the
men at Valley Forge—and I listen because I have always liked
any story about people who make great sacrifices for something
they care about. But I already know the things he is telling me.
Because when you go to school your whole life around here,
the teachers are always bringing you over to the park for a class
trip and by the time you are in eighth grade you feel like you can
say all the dates and generals' names and all the facts about that
terrible Valley Forge winter backward and forward and upside
down.

"No, I know—I mean, I don't mean to—you know—even

suggest that!" Ryan says. And now his handsome face looks so sad and so sorry I have to laugh.

"*No te preocupes,* don't worry," I assure him, squeezing his hand. He puts his arm around my waist and pulls me closer. I like him, this Ryan Sweeney. He interests me. He is handsome and sweet and because he is living at the Academy he is only free some of the time and mostly on weekends. I like that, too—just enough to have a few laughs and some good kissing but not so much that I am feeling he is always around. Not so much that it interferes with my music.

We keep walking, and when we reach the top of the ridge, we see it is a good day for birds and sailboats, and if you face to the east, you can see almost to Philadelphia. With the gentle breeze on our backs and no one else around, it is a good day for romance, too. We stand on a flat rock and we are kissing and laughing and touching each other a long time. We lie down together in the sun that is following us like a good friend, and out of Ryan's pocket comes a wallet that falls open to the photos, and oh, what have we here?

"Ooooh, she is very pretty!" I say, grabbing the wallet before he can pick it up from where it lands. Ryan's face is very red now. I have the photo of the blonde, and I'm holding it on the side of me he can't reach.

"Carmen, listen . . . that's a friend of my family's from a long time ago. That photo shouldn't even be in there! Here—give it back and I'll tear it up."

I decide to see how quick red-faced Ryan really is. I kick off my shoes and leap from rock to rock with him following me, trying to cut me off, reaching to grab my arm and missing—and me changing direction and stopping here and there to wave the photo, teasing him.

"Damn, you're quick. What are you, half leopard or something?" he pants as I leap to safety on the highest rock and make him miss again. I stick out my tongue like a child and wave the picture just beyond his reach.

"You are actually smiling, serious Ryan, do you know that?" I call down to him. He stops and holds out his arms for me to climb into. "Not yet. . . . First you tell me her name and then I tell you her fortune. Then maybe I will come down there and kiss you!"

He shakes his head, lowers his arms, and puts his hands on his hips. But he is still smiling, I can see that. He gets more handsome, too, when he is happy; but also I can see there is something inside him that says Ryan Sweeney does not deserve to have fun like every other human being.

"Well, Red?" I ask. "I am waiting here. . . . I can't tell her fortune unless you tell me her name."

Ryan hesitates. "Lauren," he says finally.

I nod. I hold the photo out at a good distance and study the face, the expression, the clothing, the makeup, the posture, the jewelry. This is not the difficult kind of fortune-telling that *mi abuela* has taught me, the kind you must practice often and have patience to learn. No. This is simply having ears and eyes when I am waiting on girls like Lauren at the counter of the Quikmart. This is too easy. Much, much too easy.

RYAN

⎯⎯•❧•⎯⎯

"Big house, expensive car and clothes, tennis-club membership, nice parties. But poor Lauren, she is not so happy with this beautiful life. She is always at Weight Watchers because she spends most of her days driving her two and a half bratty kids with smooth, pudgy hands and TVs in their bedrooms . . . driving them to their dancing lessons and soccer games and cheerleading practices. . . . Poor, poor Lauren!" Carmen looks down at me and frowns a clown's frown . . . part real, part exaggeration.

"Two and *a half* bratty kids?" I ask jokingly.

Carmen considers the photograph once more. "Two or three—I can't decide."

I pretend to be disappointed. "And here I thought you were a *real* fortune-teller," I say, shaking my head. I reach up toward her, and this time she grins, jumps into my arms, and kisses me.

"And what about you?" I ask when we finally come up for air. "What do you see in your future as far as a home and kids and a guy you can belong to?"

Carmen pushes me away suddenly. She steps back, her eyes narrowing. *"Belong to?* Is that what you said, Ryan Sweeney? *Belong to?"*

I shrug. I'm not sure what I said that has made such a dent in our romantic mood. "Well, yeah . . . but I can rephrase if you want."

Carmen keeps her distance and studies me carefully, knuckles on her hips. She's hands down the hottest girl I've ever seen. Finally, she grins and moves closer to me again.

"OK, I forgive you, Red," she says, taking my hands in her own. "But you should know this: Carmen is free. Carmen belongs to no one. Ever."

I try to listen to the words coming out of her mouth. But truthfully, right now I'd agree to anything she said. Anything. If she said, *Ryan Sweeney, walk over to that rock and throw yourself off the ledge*, I probably would. All I can do is wrap my arms around her and draw her closer, kissing her.

A group of hikers approaches from below. I slip my hands underneath her legs and carry her away from the ridge, laying her gently down under an ancient maple whose leaves are just beginning to unfurl. If you asked me to choose between food, sleep, good health, a million dollars, and Carmen's body, well . . . the choice wouldn't be hard. If you said that I, Cadet Captain Ryan Sweeney, Mr. Discipline Control Freak, would fall for a girl who made him feel like he had absolutely no control over anything . . . well, then *you'd* be the master fortune-teller. Because that's exactly what has happened.

We spend the rest of the afternoon under that tree, getting to know one another a lot better. Finally, we head back to the gate, where we catch the shuttle to the bus stop at the mall.

"I can't leave campus tomorrow . . . but is there someplace

you like where I can take you for dinner next Friday?" I ask as we wait for the number 17 to take her home. "Someplace that's not a chain," I add quickly, thinking: *Someplace where we won't run into any of the other cadets, or the general and his wife, or anyone having anything to do with the Academy.* Even though upper-classmen are allowed to date off campus, I want to keep our relationship totally separate from VFMA—separate from anything that might interfere. Because if there's anything the military knows how to do really well, it's interfere.

"Well . . . there's Placido's—if you like Italian food," she suggests.

"I'll eat anything if I can look across the table at you," I reply, wondering how the hell I'll survive the next six days without seeing her.

Carmen laughs hard at this. "Ryan Sweeney," she says, stepping forward to put her face about two centimeters from mine. "You are not always such a shy guy, are you?"

I don't have to tell you how we spend the next few minutes before her bus shows up.

After we say good-bye, I walk over to the shuttle stop and stand under the sign, waiting for Jimmy and Luke. Already, I feel like someone tore my insides out. I'm a hollow shell, the week ahead stretching before me like a dark hallway with no exit doors and only a faint glimmer of light way, way off. Glancing up to where I can see the number 17 bus turning onto the main highway from the access road, I fight the urge to run after it. (God, what's wrong with me?) The urge is so strong I have to grasp the metal sign beside me to keep myself from actually doing it.

Suddenly I'm laughing out loud, scaring the pair of gray-haired ladies standing on the other side and causing them to move closer to the security-guard station. I'm laughing as I remember looking down on all those "weak" people who become addicted to things they eat or sniff, drink or swallow. *Not me,* I would always tell myself. I could never let myself become so helpless. So single-minded. So possessed. No. Not me—not Cadet Captain Ryan Sweeney.

Ha! What a load of crap that was! (I'm laughing again. The ladies are clutching their handbags, exchanging worried looks.) I'm an addict, all right. I am spent. Helpless. I am a worthless wretch. I would do anything—yes, anything at all—to be with Carmen. To hold her, to smell her, to kiss her. I might as well be lying on the sidewalk somewhere, filthy and half conscious, clutching a bottle hidden inside a brown paper bag, calling out to passersby, begging for a few bucks so I can buy another drink.

The sound of footsteps draws me back into the present. Jimmy and Luke are sprinting toward me just as the shuttle arrives. I pull myself together, release my grip on the signpost, straighten my posture. Of course, to maintain some respect, I point condemningly to my watch and give them a little tongue-lashing before I hustle them to their seats.

The whole ride back, they jabber on about their three hours of freedom at the mall. But I'm not listening. I close my eyes, lean back, and remember how she looked up there on that rock with the sun shining behind her like a golden crown, her laughter raining down.

WILL

This thing with Ryan and Carmen is starting to tick me off. I'm not sure why, but it is. I guess it's mostly because we were always a team—always doing stuff together when we had free time on campus or permission to leave. But that's changed ever since he met her.

After shooting around with some of the guys in the gym, I get cleaned up and ride into town beside Sergeant O'Connor, but I'm still thinking about it. I try to be honest with myself about the whole thing: Does it bother me that he has a girl he's really into? No. Not really. I mean, Ryan is behind most of us in the girl-experience category. He deserves it. So what is it, then? I guess I just miss having my best friend around—and I mean that literally and figuratively, because he's not himself, even when he's physically here (today playing basketball is a perfect example). It's like someone kidnapped his soul or something. It's weird.

I try to forget about it while Sergeant O'Connor and I pick up supplies at the grocery store, the UPS shipping place, and the pharmacy. Fortunately, he's getting in the habit of taking me along on his supply runs. And since I know this is his only chance to buy lottery tickets, he doesn't hesitate when I suggest we stop at the Quikmart before heading back. Once we're inside, all I have to do is wait for him to be occupied with inking in all the little ovals on the Powerball lottery ticket. I just slip around back, retrieve the box of cigarettes, put it under a blanket in the truck, and come back inside the store. He just assumes I'm somewhere in the aisles and doesn't even notice I'm gone.

This time, just like last week, the box is exactly where Carmen said it would be. That's good. It means she's reliable. Which is really important, now that my contraband source is off campus. It makes logistics a little harder, the whole transaction a little more risky.

"What can I get for you today?" the girl behind the deli counter asks me once I'm back inside. *Maggie.* Carmen let me know that when she isn't here, I can trust Maggie, same as I would her. I move closer to the counter.

"Well . . . I already got what I came for," I tell her. She nods that she understands.

"But a roast beef and Swiss with brown mustard would be great," I add.

"White or wheat roll?"

"Wheat," I say.

I step away again while Maggie makes the sandwich. Sergeant O'Connor has picked his lucky numbers and is paying the large man behind the counter. He catches my eye, motions with his hand that we should be heading back.

"There you go," Maggie says, putting the wrapped sandwich on top of the counter. "You pay up front."

I nod my thanks. "Say hello to your friend for me. . . . I think she's with my friend."

Maggie giggles. "*Sí*, yeah. They are together. For now, anyway."

I pay for my early supper, step outside, and slide into the passenger seat next to O'Connor. A quick glance over my left shoulder confirms the box shape bulging beneath the blanket.

"I saw you talking to that deli girl," O'Connor informs me as we turn onto the main road. "You know, Martens, if you're gonna go after one of the townies, there's another counter girl who wasn't there today, but oooooh boy, she's somethin' else. Too young for me, but for a kid like you . . . ," the sergeant says, thinking he's doing me a real favor imparting some adult male wisdom.

"Is that so, sir?" I reply. "Well, I guess I'll just have to come back with you next time and have a look." He smiles widely, reveling in this rare opportunity to mentor me in the fine art of the female pickup.

I turn quickly to look out the window so he can't see me almost burst out laughing. As we drive through the center of town, passing the quaint little coffee shops and boutiques, I'm just imagining what Ryan would do if he heard what O'Connor said about Carmen.

VFMA

April 16, 2007

Dear Adam,

    Hey, I'm sorry it's taken me a few weeks to write back to you. You know how it is here—class, drill, parade, inspection, homework, chapel . . . with a little eating and sleeping thrown in. Though I'm sure you wouldn't mind being back here, right? This would all seem like R & R to you. To tell you the truth, I've been putting off writing to you because I wasn't sure I had anything interesting to say. But then, well . . . I met this girl. Not like the girls from home or the ones I kind of knew from prep school. She's really different. Special. (I can hear your first question even across the ocean: Yes, she is hot.) Anyway, whenever I can get off campus, I try and see her. So—I guess that's another reason I've been a pretty poor correspondent. It's going real well so far.

    Anyway, enough about me. The younger guys in A Company, the ones who know that you're over there, they're always asking me what it's really like. We all watch the news when we can, and of course, we get the ten-second sound bites from Fox or CNN on our computers. And the general is always making it sound like we're about a month away from declaring Baghdad a second Philadelphia—with brotherhood, liberty, and equal rights for all. But from your most recent letter, I guess it's not going all that great, and I guess that must make you really tired. I mean, it's one thing to put your ass on the line day after day if you're moving forward. But when you're not . . .

OK, on a lighter note, Will remains the Will Martens you know from home. We're still tight, but we don't hang out as much when we have leave—mostly 'cause of me and Carmen (that's the girl I was telling you about). Will's playing really good basketball, and he's holding his own in the classroom, too, so my guess is he's a definite for a college scholarship somewhere. In the meantime, he keeps one foot in the real world and gets away with what he can.

Gotta go. Today's our annual open house, so I'll be giving tours, holding doors, and generally being a shining example of all we hold true and dear here at the V. But I guess there are worse ways to spend a Sunday. . . .

Hang in there, big bro—and bring your indestructible self home as soon as you can.

Your not-so-stupid kid brother,
Ryan

MAGGIE

On Tuesday, Carmen is skipping across the street like a little girl and coming to ask me *Maggeeeee!*—we need pictures of the band to send to New York, so can you come to Lenny's tonight and bring your brother's good camera with the big lenses and maybe you can help us with lights and how to pose?

And of course, I know about this picture stuff already from Lenny, but I am jumping around the room and skipping, too, because why not? This is very good news for Carmen and the band. While she is calling Lenny to be sure all the guys can be there and also telling me her ideas for how the band should pose in these photos, I reach into my backpack and pull out the test I got back this week at Vo-Tech with the amazing A-minus at the top and *Good job* next to that in big letters with the red pen of Mr. Hornbeck, my teacher.

"*¡Vaya!* That's great! You are smart, my sister!" Carmen cries when she is off the phone. She tapes the test to my bedroom mirror and writes *S-M-A-R-T* beneath my name in big pencil letters.

She borrows a few things from my makeup kit while I am cleaning the lenses and adjusting the settings on Raúl's camera, which he won in a poker game but never uses. We get Marco to drive us over to Lenny's and on the way I ask Carmen about her date at the park with Ryan Sweeney and did she tell him this time that he is not her priority.

"He was handsome and not so shy with me this time," she tells me as she fixes her hair and puts on some eye makeup for the pictures. We are stopped in traffic by the mall and she is looking in the little mirror on the back of the visor and Marco is watching her as she strokes on the black eyeliner and silver-tinged eye shadow. This makes her already big eyes seem even bigger and even greener and this will look very good I think in the pictures.

"I like him, Maggie, but already he is wanting to make dates with me every weekend, and he is always trying to call me in between. And even though he is good-looking and also an excellent kisser, I think maybe now that the man from the studio in New York is asking for our photo and is coming down to see us again the next time we play at Gallagher's . . . I think maybe I will have to tell Ryan Sweeney I am too busy with my music to see him."

Marco shakes his head in disbelief, just like Mami does when my brothers come in too late from the bars. "Beautiful women . . . they are *mala suerte*. Bad luck. Always taking our hearts and"— he takes the empty soda can from his cup holder, lifts it in his right hand above the dashboard, and closes his fist—"crushing them like a ripe orange!" He grins mischievously, dropping the crushed can at Carmen's feet.

Carmen and me, we are laughing hard at this gesture from Marco, who is the most softhearted of my brothers and also the most unlucky in love. We are laughing because we know what Marco says is true. And while we are laughing, I am asking myself if it is only beautiful women who do this, because I am not one of them. I look at the crushed can at Carmen's feet and I think maybe, once in a while, it is not so bad to be plain.

•

CARMEN

We get to Lenny's after the others, and Jorge says he has a friend to cover for him at work but only till eight o'clock and please can we do these quick so he can get back before the boss finds out. I tell Lenny about the ideas me and Maggie have for how to set up the pictures, and Lenny (who looks really good tonight in his new black shirt and boots) writes them down and makes a small sketch for each one with our names where we should sit or stand.

"OK, Maggie," Lenny says, handing her the sketches. "You're the director. Tell us where we should be."

Maggie looks at the first sketch and she arranges each of us just so against the background (a pale blue sheet taped up on one of Lenny's living-room walls). She takes the shades off two floor lamps and leans the lamps against the back of Lenny's couch, aiming the bulbs toward us so it's like we are in a real photography studio with spotlights. She takes a few photos—then moves Jorge to the left and Nick to the right and *flash, flash, flash* she takes a few more. After this, she moves the lamps, and we all have to arrange ourselves on the couch like in the next sketch, and she says: "Carmen, you hold that heart-shaped pillow on your lap. ¡*Perfecto!* That looks good." *Click, click, click. Flash, flash.* I try to hold as still as I can, but it's hard because while

Maggie is refocusing, the phone inside my jean-skirt pocket begins to vibrate, and Nick, who is sitting right next to me, can feel it, too. He starts to laugh and so does Lenny and then, finally, Jorge does, too. We all fall off of the couch in a big heap and we are saying to Maggie, "Wait!" I reach into my pocket and grab the phone and *ay*—not again—it is Ryan trying to call me and I snap the phone shut but I don't turn it off because what if *mis abuelos* have some kind of trouble and I do not answer?

"*Lo siento*—sorry!" I tell everyone. We all get back into our places on the couch, and Maggie takes this picture from three or four different angles before she says, "OK, got it," and we can move again.

Next, we all go to the kitchen for the picture that is my idea: a casual look—us around the table, with Nick stubbing his cigarette in an ashtray and Jorge and me playing our guitars and Lenny beating out the rhythm on the tabletop like we are all working together on a new song.

"*Sí—perfecto*," Maggie says. "Hold it there. A little more relaxed faces—*bueno*—that's better."

We move out to the garage for the final photos. The lights out there are not so bright, but Lenny, he thinks fast and points the headlights from his brothers' dirt bikes right on us and Maggie says: "OK, these will work very good, but try hard not to squint." Everyone plays through two songs, and Maggie takes candids of each of us separately and then all of us together. During the second song, I can feel my phone shaking again inside my pocket and after we stop playing I check it and see the text **can u talk?** from Ryan. I erase it and tuck the phone back in my skirt.

We are done before eight o'clock so Jorge can jump into his

Toyota pickup and speed off to his job before the boss notices. Nick, Lenny, Maggie, and me, we go inside to eat chips and salsa and share a six-pack of Miller Lite. Maggie is showing us in the little preview screen in back of the camera how the photos came out, and we are all telling her how good they are and maybe we shouldn't just pick one or two but maybe send five or six to New York.

"A toast to the Gypsy Lovers!" Lenny says, holding his bottle high over the kitchen table. "And to Maggie, who is patient and clever and makes us look good." We raise our bottles to meet Lenny's and Maggie is smiling big and I see how much she is enjoying this compliment. I take a long drink and when I put my bottle down Lenny is looking at me and grinning, and maybe it's because of the beer, but I notice in the dim light of the kitchen how adorable he is.

RYAN

Why does she do this? I know she sees my number on the caller ID. She *knows* it's me. Why doesn't she answer? Doesn't she know how badly I need to hear her voice (which still makes my knees go weak), to hear her say she *wants* to see me again, that she thinks about me when we can't be together?

Hola, this is Carmen—leave a message after the beep.

Damn! Why does she do this?

At first, I thought it was great to have a girlfriend on the "outside" (well, actually—here at the V, we don't have a choice about that). But you know what I mean . . . a girl who could be a nice distraction from campus life—from all the rules, drills, and regulations inside these cold walls. Yeah, at first I really liked that.

But then I realized (God, what an *idiot* I am!) how sexy she is—and that other guys see her that way, too. That day she gave me the rose—and again that next time at Gallagher's—it was like I took my first dose of a too-potent drug that I'd be hooked on forever.

After being with her at the park, I can't stop thinking, can't stop imagining, what might be happening between her and all the other guys out there. Are they staring? Whistling? Flirting?

Are they making her smile and laugh? Are they wanting to hold her and kiss her like I do?

Maybe she's free now. Maybe her phone was just out of range. . . .

Hola, *this is Carmen—leave a message after the beep.*

Dammit! Why does she do this?

WILL

At dinner, they announce that we should all report to the chapel afterward for a mandatory meeting. This happened twice already this year—and both times it was some big announcement about the Iraq War. Some of our alums getting honored—or killed (and in General Hirshman's eyes, there's no difference). So of course, we assume tonight will be more of the same. But instead, it's just some guy from the Pentagon (he'd fought with the general in Vietnam) who wants to lecture us while he's passing through Philadelphia on his way back to Washington.

You can just imagine how thrilled we all are. . . . We sit in those cold, hard pews for what feels like an eternity, listening to him drone on about "our superior intelligence-gathering capabilities" and the "ever-increasing threat of radical fundamentalist terrorists," blah, blah, blah. All stuff we can get from the Internet or from any of the newspaper headlines. But of course, then *he* wouldn't get his generous speaking fee—and probably a brandy or two and some imported cigars at the general's house afterward.

When he finishes his speech, we all stand and applaud like mad, mostly because we are so glad it's over. Ryan and I walk out with a bunch of plebes from A Company, and when they turn off the main path toward their dorm, I figure it's as good a time as any to tell my roommate what's on my mind.

"I gotta tell you, Ry—some of the guys are worried about you," I say, slowing my pace so that we're not within earshot of anyone else.

Ryan looks straight ahead and keeps walking. No change in his expression.

"After that—uh—incident—with Vanderkamp, and the failed inspections, showing up late for drill and parade . . ." We keep walking. Ryan kicks at a neatly swept pile of branches that the gardener left at the edge of the sidewalk. They scatter across the grass like some kid's game of pickup sticks. He doesn't respond, but I press on.

"And, hey, I'm no Einstein, but I couldn't help but notice those Fs on your science and philosophy tests. I mean . . . what gives, Ry? Is all this because of some chick? I mean"—I quickly amend that word—"is Carmen causing all this? Because it seems like you're giving up a lot more for her than a few half-court games of basketball. And in the meantime, everyone's noticing how you've changed. Everyone's asking me what's going on with you."

Ryan shoves his hands deeper into his pockets. He speeds up a bit, then slows down again, having decided, I guess, not to ignore me entirely.

"And, so . . . what are you telling them?"

"Nothing. I'm telling them *nothing*, Ry, that's the whole problem." I swing around in front of him and block his path. He stops, and we stand there face to face, the many years of friendship swinging between us like a fragile glass pendulum. "They have eyes and ears, you know. They're not stupid. They see that you're not the same Ryan Sweeney they've gotten used to."

Ryan frowns and looks down, then across the quad toward the main entrance, where the almost-full moon illuminates the cadet guards, the high brick pillars, the shiny iron gate. On the opposite side, the silvery ribbon of road beckons toward town. I can't tell if he's remembering the night he fought with Kamp, or if he's wishing he was just the hell out of here. Either way, he owes me an answer. I wait.

"If I could explain it to you, Will, I would," he says at last. "I know this thing with me and Carmen has been—you know—complicated. I know you're covering for me sometimes—and I appreciate it, I really do. But . . . I can't stop seeing her. I'd see her more often if I could. I feel like . . ." He pauses, searches the dark sky for the right words. "I feel like I've been locked in this dark room for a long time . . . and now all of a sudden someone's opened the door and lifted the shades and I can really breathe and I can see things that I didn't even know existed."

If you had told me a month ago that Ryan Sweeney would be waxing poetic in the middle of the Academy quad, I'd have said you were nuts. But here he is, and here I am, and what can I say?

"I know it's hard for you to understand," he continues as we turn and resume walking toward the dorm. "But just hang in there with me, OK?"

We reach the building after ten p.m., when the security system automatically kicks in. As I fumble around in my pocket

for the key card to let us in, I notice a pair of bright green eyes staring at me from the bush beside the door. Probably one of the local
raccoons or possums—little smugglers who come and go as they
please, able to creep through the smallest opening to steal a half
sandwich here, a discarded candy bar there, before slipping back
to the real world.

Part 5

Carmen will always be free.

Gypsy she was born, Gypsy she will die.

ॐ *Prosper Mérimée, CARMEN*

RYAN

"Beauty," says Major Breyer, strolling up and down the rows, his hands gesturing like a conductor's. "How do we define it? How do we know it when we see it, when we hear it?" I'm sitting in philosophy, a class I used to enjoy but lately have found myself fighting to keep awake in. A class that—at four-thirty on a Friday, a mere two hours before my dinner with Carmen—requires way too much gray matter.

The major closes the windows, shutting out the late-April sunshine, the smell of freshly mowed grass on the quad. Dimming the lights, he shows us slides of the Sistine Chapel ceiling, a self-portrait by Frida Kahlo, da Vinci's *Mona Lisa*, Rodin's *The Thinker*, and Monet's *Water Lilies*. Then we see photographs of ancient trees by Ansel Adams and a few of the Alvin Ailey dancers caught midleap. Yesterday we *listened* for beauty: excerpts from Joplin (Janis *and* Scott), Beethoven, some instrumental bluegrass, Springsteen, and Beyoncé.

I'm with him for a while, but somewhere between da Vinci and Monet, the major loses me. My mind drifts to Carmen and to that first time I saw her behind the checkout counter at the Quikmart. How different she was from all those girls in glossy photos on the magazine covers: platinum blondes with penciled-on eyebrows and way too much makeup, every one of them stamped out like mannequins. I guess I used to think they were beautiful, too.

But that was before Carmen's olive skin, her deep green eyes, her smile that made my heart race. And that hair! Blacker than a raven's, blacker than a moonless winter night, blacker than my saber's leather sheath. (And somehow, with all that darkness, she seems radiant, wrapped in light.) That first day, as she punched numbers into the Quikmart register, the snake tattooed on her wrist poised to strike, I stood there like I was frozen. I couldn't take my eyes off her. And when she finally looked up, I swear, it was like I was struck by lightning. I shudder now, remembering that moment.

"Mr. Sweeney. Are you all right?" Major Breyer stands beside me, peering over his spectacles, his eyebrows arched in concern. "You're shaking. Are you ill?"

"Yes sir. . . . I mean, no sir." I look down at my hand on the desk and will it to stillness. "I'm fine. Just—er, um, a little tired, I guess."

"He's contemplating beauty, sir," Will offers, grinning at me knowingly from across the room. A conspiratorial chuckle ripples through the class. Major Breyer, however, is in no mood for jokes.

"Well, then you're all in luck," he announces, moving away from my desk and toward the blackboard. "I'm going to provide you with an opportunity to contemplate the notion of beauty for a while longer." He scrawls the prompt for a thousand-word essay on the subject, then drops the chalk dramatically onto his desk. "Due Monday, no exceptions! Good day, gentlemen."

Twenty-one guys eject themselves from their chairs and head for the door. I'm only three steps from the door myself when Major Breyer intercepts me.

"Mr. Sweeney! I'll expect a top-notch essay from you on Monday. Given your recent work in this class, you're going to need at *least* that to pass."

I snap instinctively to attention, giving the major my most dignified salute.

"Yes sir, Major Breyer. You can count on it, sir."

He pauses, starts to say something else, then sighs, returns my salute, and lets me pass.

Will's waiting in the hall and we head for the stairs together. "I guess since you're still, um—occupied—on weekends, you won't be able to help me with this paper, right?" he asks.

I shove him halfheartedly into the statue of Eisenhower that stands on the second-floor landing. He laughs and bows mockingly at the bronze general. "Please excuse my friend here, sir. He's just . . . you know . . . a little lovesick!"

Outside, we turn left and head across the quad. "Kantor, MacAdoo, Doyle, Michaels, and me—we're meeting for some basketball at five," Will says. "Doyle challenged the G Company plebes and they accepted. You're comin', right?"

"Nope. Can't," I tell him. "I gotta get cleaned up and meet Carmen. I'm taking her to some Italian place."

Will stops walking. He grabs my elbow and pulls me back. "Ry . . . listen . . . it's Friday. Aside from drill and guard duty,

you got the whole goddamn weekend to see your girl." Will
pleads: "C'mon, Ry. Five o'clock. I already told them you were in."
    I shrug. I've been counting the hours till I see her again, and
no pickup game of basketball is going to prevent it. "Then tell
them you were wrong. I'm not in. Not today anyway, but—"
    "*Fine,*" Will interrupts. "Go ahead and have your hot date."
He spits on the grass. "So I guess we shouldn't count on you joining us later, either, right?"
    I shrug again, a gesture that's become my default response to
Will and almost everyone else these past several weeks. My best
friend turns away quickly. He runs to catch up with a group of guys
heading across the quad. I continue alone, with only the memory
of Carmen's laugh for company.

CARMEN

Like a cougar after a full meal. Abuelo used to say this is how I slept as a child—very hard and right away, as soon as I was feeling tired. And even now, this is how I sleep almost always. But tonight *¡ay Señor!* I cannot sleep! I don't know, but I think maybe I am a little bit nervous about next Saturday when the man from the studio in New York City is coming to hear us at Gallagher's with his boss. This is my big dream and what if . . . ? *¡Dios mío!* I must chase these bad thoughts from my head. They are invisible and annoying—like mosquitoes in July. I try to close my eyes and rest, but after one hour of this I give up.

I slip downstairs to the Cave, quiet as fog. I light some candles and sit on the Dragon with my guitar. I strum the strings softly so I don't wake *mis abuelos*. This week I am writing many lines in my notebook and now I must find the right chords to go with them. I think here in these pages I have another good song—but I must capture it while the emotions are fresh.

I am playing for I don't know how long, and here comes Baji appearing from out of the dark. She curls up beside me and now I know I will have a song tonight because Baji is always bringing me luck. I sing to her softly this new song about a soldier who has lost his way home and then he meets a Gypsy, and we don't know if he finds his way again or is lost forever. And yes, of course I know this song is because of Ryan Sweeney; so it is making me a little bit sad that soon I will have to tell him I am too busy with my music to see him anymore.

I stay in the Cave playing this new song over and over. By the time the candles are burned low and there is one thin beam of sun streaming in from the little window near the furnace, I think it is finished. I kiss my guitar, *mi vieja amiga*, my old friend, and place it gently down on the Dragon so my hands can be free.

My lucky deck feels cool in my palm. I sit on the floor turning the cards around and around before spreading them in a half circle before me. I draw three cards and pull them close to me, pushing the others away. First card: the ace of diamonds. (Ah— my possessions may increase. That is good.) Second card: the three of clubs. (This is good, too! There will be a helpful person or event.) Third card: the seven of spades. (*¡Ay!* This is bad. It means beware of treachery—or even betrayal.)

I take a deep breath, cross my chest. I say one Our Father, two Hail Marys. I make sure all the candles are out. I open the little window so Baji can leave when she wants. Then I walk upstairs to make breakfast for *mis abuelos.*

RYAN

"You take the number five bus from the mall to the stop on Lancaster Avenue, just before Villanova," Carmen explained when she finally returned one of my calls. "Walk two blocks up from the stop and you'll see Placido's on your right. . . . I will meet you there. . . . Six-thirty."

I arrive at six-fifteen, a little early, which is just how I'd planned. I want this dinner to be special—a night she won't soon forget. I stand outside and study the brightly painted mural across the front of the building: a collage of Italian scenes including the Leaning Tower of Pisa, the Roman Colosseum, and a country vineyard with pretty girls stomping grapes in a giant wooden barrel. Peering through the windows, I see that the tables are small and far apart, with flickering candles and fresh flowers. Perfect.

I step inside and ask the fiftyish mustached maître d' where the most private table is located.

"All of our tables are private!" he says somewhat indignantly, sweeping his hand across the one large room and the smaller area I can see at the far end, separated by a pair of small swinging doors. I look around at the people who are already seated—all dressed casually, but fairly *nice* casual. This looks like a place that people come back to, a place that fills up easily and doesn't need to cater to a new face, especially one as young as mine.

Luckily, I anticipated this. I feel around in my pocket behind the little jewelry box and whip out the twenty I've stashed just for such an occasion. Quickly I swing around the guy's podium so that I'm looking down at his seating chart, each table neatly represented with a small black numbered square.

"How about when my date comes, you give me that table . . . *there?*" I ask him, plopping my twenty down and pointing to one of the two squares in the little back room at the edge of the diagram. He looks at me quizzically, as if trying to determine if I'm serious. I lift my hand, leaving the bill on the stand, thinking how lucky I am that Mom thinks we don't get enough to eat at the V and sends me an extra forty bucks a month—cash.

Just then the door opens and in comes Carmen, dressed in a tight-fitting bright yellow dress and silver heels. That freight train rumbles through my chest again, and I wonder if one of these times my heart just might explode when I look at her. She smiles when she sees me.

"Am I late?" she asks.

The maître d' is staring at her. Specifically, he's staring at her chest. He doesn't even try to hide it. I nudge his arm with my elbow. "So . . . how 'bout that table?"

Quicker than you can say "dirty old Italian man," he slides my twenty up his sleeve, gathers up two menus, and leads my girl and me through the swinging doors to a table in the back room.

CARMEN

At home, I am looking in the mirror at the dark circles under my eyes, and I think about calling Ryan Sweeney to tell him I am too tired for our dinner at Placido's. But then I think he will just keep calling me again, and *No, Carmen,* I tell myself, *tonight you must tell him how it is with you, how you need to have more time for your music.* So then when I am getting dressed, I call Lenny and tell him I have written this new song and maybe it is good enough even for playing next Saturday at Gallagher's. I sing one verse for him and he says, "Why don't you come over tonight after eight. . . . Nick will be here, too, and we'll work on the arrangement," and I say, "*Sí,* OK, I'll see you later."

Now in this little room where Ryan has paid extra (I saw that green slide up the sleeve of the old man!), I am feeling very tired but also excited for Lenny and Nick to hear my new song. I am smiling at my date, but I am not really listening to something he is telling me about his philosophy class and some guys named Alvin and Ansel, which sounds like a weird fairy tale to me.

". . . the colonel caught me, though, and he almost held me after. I'm not doing so well lately in that class," Ryan says, and takes something out of his pocket. It's a very small jewelry

box—the pretty kind, with blue velvet on the outside—and he is
sliding it across the table toward me. *¡Dios mío!* No gifts for me
now—no! I don't want anything from you, can't you see that, you
innocent, red-faced boy? (*Ay* . . . what trouble a rose and a few
good kisses can bring!)

And of course I am thinking this inside my head, but on the
outside I am trying not to hurt his feelings so much. But OK, now
I must tell him how it is.

"Red . . ."(He still blushes when I call him this.) "Do you
remember how I told you about my dream of being—"

"Go ahead and open it!" he interrupts, pushing the little blue
velvet box closer to my hand. He is squirming a little in his chair
and now this makes me feel nervous, too. (How can I tell this boy
I do not want to see him anymore? He is not like other boys I
know: someone has made him too hard on the outside, so that inside, his heart is very soft. But I must take hold of my life. . . . My
music is what I love and not this Ryan Sweeney. *¡Ay!* This will not
be easy.)

"Ryan," I say, looking straight at his face and reaching across
the table to take his hand, just like I did that first night at Gallagher's. "*Lo siento.* Forgive me. I cannot take this gift from you. I
cannot take it because even though I like you and we have had
some fun together, I need more time for my music, for my dream.
That is what is most important to me now."

Ryan looks at me but he says nothing. Finally, he takes my
other hand in his. "That's cool. No problem," he says. "I can't see
you during the week anyhow—at least until school's out. But then
in the summer, I can get a job up here . . . close by . . . and we

can see each other all the time and I'll take you to the beach and—"

"*No!*" I say, and drop his hands on the table. This boy has made plans for me, and that makes me angry. Now it is not so hard to say what is on my mind. "No!" I repeat. "You were not listening to me! *Listen:* I am too busy now for these dates. I am too busy for these plans. Too busy for all of your little phone calls and messages. This is *my* time and *my* life and I need to be free."

I stand up quickly and push in the chair. I see now the waiter is coming toward our room and I want to leave before he reaches us.

"Good-bye, Ryan. Thank you for the song you gave me. But you and I, soldier boy, we are over. Done."

I hurry through the swinging doors, past the waiter with the surprise on his face, past the mustache at the desk, out the front door and onto the street. I kick off my heels and sweep them into my hands. I run many blocks before I stop near the front gate of Villanova University, where the statue of Mother Mary welcomes me.

RYAN

It takes my brain a while to realize what just happened. The waiter is on his way to the table, but after he takes one look at me, he pivots on his heels and leaves. Good choice. I'm sure I look as bad as I feel. Bad. *How* bad? *Real* bad. Super bad. Bad-bad. For about thirty seconds, I consider ramming the steak knife from my place setting straight into my chest. Just ending it.

But then—I sit there, talking to myself. I replay the last six or seven minutes—and then the last six or seven weeks. And that's when I realize I have to get a grip, because I just made the classic mistake of a guy who's not spent a lot of time around girls: I pushed too hard. I went too fast. I should have taken it slower . . . should have let her have more space. Yeah, that's it. She's just scared, that's all. I mean, God, the way she looks at me—the way she kisses me—that isn't make-believe, is it? No. It's all been real—and all good. She likes me, all right. She just needs some time off. We're cool, me and Carmen. She's just running scared. I'll give her a few days to chill, and then I'll call her and we'll make up.

I feel better now. I reach across the table and open the little velvet box with the ring inside—a small rosebud-shaped stone, blood-red and shiny. I know that when the time is right, it will look perfect on her hand.

CARMEN

Like a hawk tied to a perch. Like a hobbled horse. Like a fish taken from the river and thrown into a bowl. On the bus back from Villanova, I close my eyes and I realize that is how I was feeling with Ryan.

But now I am free again. Free! I know maybe sometimes I will think about his handsome smile, his soft touch on my face, the way he would blush whenever I called him Red. Yes, of course I will. We only went out a few times, but we had some fun, didn't we? It is nice to have someone to hold and to talk to late at night or to kiss on a warm afternoon in the park.

But now I am finished with this cadet. And if this is a big surprise for him, well—that is too bad. It is too bad because on that day we spent together in Valley Forge Park, I *told* him how it was with me. I told him that Carmen does not belong to anyone. Yes, I said this from the very beginning. (Well, *claro*, *almost* from the very beginning. But at least I *told* him. I did not lie.) And what did I get in return for my honesty? Too many phone calls interrupting my life; a gift (a small box—I think it was a ring) I did not ask for and did not want. And yes, it is true: one very good song and maybe now a second one. But also a very big distraction from my music. Conflict and worry, just like the cards predicted. The nine of spades: conflict and worry.

   So now I am free. No more invisible leash around my neck and phone calls always wanting to know where I am and what I'm doing and *Carmen, Carmen, say you think about me, say you miss me. ¡Ay!* My heart belongs to *mis abuelos*. And to Maggie, who is like my sister. And my music. They are enough for me now. And if I choose to smile at another boy and to let him put his arm around my waist and kiss me . . . well, that is my choice. I am free to do as I please. I am no dog on a leash. No hobbled horse or pretty fish in a bowl. Ryan Sweeney, my red-faced boy, my shy cadet—I am glad I am through with you. *Adiós.* Good-bye.

MAGGIE

———❧———

It is seven-thirty on Saturday night and I am singing to WYSP radio in my room and cleaning out my closet. This is something I am enjoying after a long week at Vo-Tech and working at Quikmart almost every night because at last I have this free time with no studies and no Fat Frank. And also there is the thirty dollars in my pocket cashed from my paycheck that maybe I will use at the mall this weekend for a new skirt or jewelry or shoes. (The rest, like always, I put in my account for college, but this week I reach a balance of two thousand dollars—and I say to myself, *Maggie, you deserve a little reward for this, yes?*)

Today it is almost up to eighty degrees, and if you stand on the street long enough, you can see the leaves on the trees, and the flowers in the little pots on the steps are really opening. So *hasta luego* to all my sweaters, long pants, and boots, and *bienvenidos*, welcome, to my sandals and tanks and cutoffs. And now the DJ must be thinking the same as me, because right on cue he is playing "California Girls" by the Beach Boys and I am singing along so loud that Marco comes by in the hall with his hands on his ears and his eyes rolling around in their sockets like pinballs. He is just teasing me, I know. But even so, I turn down the radio because maybe Mami is tired after her week, too, and she is wanting to rest before she has to stay up late and yell at my brothers. And now *¡qué molestia!* some other song is interfering. I turn the dial on the radio to find the signal again. But the radio is fine, and now I see that other sound is my cell phone, and why is Carmen calling me when she is supposed to be with that cadet at a fancy restaurant?

"*¿Qué pasó?* Carmen. Why aren't you with Ryan?"

"Maggeeeee! I am home but I need to go to Lenny's to play my new song for him and Nick. So you want to come, and can Marco drive us there in fifteen minutes?"

And see, this is what I know about Carmen: she heard my question and will answer me when she is ready. "Hold on," I tell her, and yell to my softhearted brother.

"Marco! You can drive me and Carmen to Lenny's in fifteen minutes, OK?"

Marco reappears at my door with his hands still on his ears. "I can't hear you, little sister! *¿Qué dijiste?*" But Marco, he is grinning and he is already dressed to go out to the bars and flirt with girls, and so I know he will take us.

"*Sí*, Marco will take us. Fifteen minutes," I tell Carmen.

I look at all the clothes across my bed that I was planning to fold and store neatly in my dresser drawers, but now I have to hurry and get dressed to go to Lenny's, and later I will probably have to sleep underneath all of these sweaters and pants. But that is what it's like when you are best friends with Carmen: you think your day will go one way and *bang*—just like that—it goes another.

WILL

So after we annihilate the G Company plebes in three games (and yours truly, at shooting guard, averaging seventeen points a game, is hands down the MVP), I jog back to the dorm and get cleaned up. I guess I'm adjusting to not having Ry playing forward for our A Company team. But after the games, I admit, it feels weird to come back to an empty room and not be making plans to head out together and do something with the rest of the guys.

So I'm sitting on the bed, reliving the winning shot of our last game (a three-pointer from the perimeter—*swoosh!* nothing but net . . .) and cutting the athletic tape off my right ankle, when I notice the official-looking envelope sticking out of Ryan's waste-basket. "Dean's Office, VFMA" is stamped in bold blue letters in one corner. The envelope's addressed to Cadet Captain Ryan Sweeney. I hesitate—but only for a minute—before I open it and read what's inside:

> *Cadet Captain Sweeney:*
> *This letter is to inform you that as of April 25th, your GPA for the current semester is 1.75. In addition, you are receiving a failing grade in the following courses:*

*Philosophy 200 and History 245. The deans and faculty
at Valley Forge Military Academy take great pride in
the achievements of our students, and we hold those
students accountable for their academic growth and
performance. Therefore, I must also inform you that if
you fail either or both of these courses for the spring term,
you will be put on academic probation and—until the
course requirements are met—will be excluded from
VFMA in the fall.*

Sincerely,
Major Franklin Adare
Dean of the Faculty, VFMA

There is a smaller, handwritten note stapled to the letter:

*Ryan: Let's talk about this. I'm available all next
week anytime between 3 and 5 p.m.*

Major Adare

Then I notice another neatly typed line at the very bottom of
the letter:

cc: Colonel Michael Sweeney, Springfield, PA

RYAN

According to one of the plebes standing guard at the gate, Will and the other guys in A Company have already left to get dinner at the mall and to see the nine o'clock showing of *Spider-Man 3*. Which is a lucky break for yours truly, 'cause I'm in no mood to explain why I'm back early and what happened between me and Carmen.

Our floor is quiet; except for one cadet at the end of the hall who's recovering from the stomach flu, no one's around. I go straight to our room, take off my good shirt and khakis, put on my sweats, and collapse on the bed. I repeat the mantra I kept up all the way back on the bus: *We're OK. She's just scared. She'll come around.* But as many times as I repeated it, there was another small, nagging voice inside my head that said: *She's gone for good. She's not coming back. It's over.*

Now, as I lie here alone, those voices are battling. And when the second one threatens, I can feel my palms sweat, my heart pound, my throat close up. It's as if without Carmen (at the mere *thought* of being without Carmen), I become panicky and half crazed. I hate how I feel. But I can't help it. I have to do something. I have to fight back. Yes. Fight back. I'm a soldier, for Christ's sake, right? That's what soldiers do! *Think, Ryan, think. Logic and discipline have always been your strength. Use them now—use them to win her back.*

CARMEN

Marco is a good brother. He is always doing nice things for Maggie and me. Tonight, before I get into his Honda, I take a few of the big vanilla cookies that Abuelita has baked fresh and I put them in a bag for him.

It is not a far ride to Lenny's, so we are there by eight-thirty. Marco pulls away slow from the curb with his window rolled down and one of the big cookies in his mouth. We walk toward Lenny's porch and we wave *gracias, Marco!* and I know Maggie is saying a silent prayer to Mary that her softhearted brother does not come home with a black eye and bloody nose and whiskey on his breath.

The guys are talking in the living room when we come in. Maggie points to the bookcase with all the trophies from Lenny's quarterback days, and there must be more than a dozen of them—plus some pictures of him in shoulder pads and throwing a pass, which makes us laugh because *claro* it is Lenny's face but he looks so different and more like a skinny little boy back then.

Lenny clears a spot on the couch for me and Maggie and sits down on the floor (he is always polite like that). We are talking among us a little bit about this and that, and then Nick, he says to

Lenny, "Tell her," and then I say to Lenny, "Tell me what?" And then Lenny, he says, "I got a call from the guy in New York. He's definitely coming next Saturday and he's definitely bringing his boss and he really liked the photos we sent. He says if Gary—that's the boss's name—if Gary likes what he sees and hears at Gallagher's, then he will sit down with us after the show and we'll talk about a recording contract. . . ."

Of course when Lenny is saying these words "recording contract," I am getting shivers down my back. And then I am springing up from that couch and so is Maggie and we are being a little crazy with our squealing and jumping up and down and hugging each other. Then I am pulling the boys up from the floor and hugging them, too, and Lenny, he kisses me quick on the neck so that my shoulders get shivery again. And after this, the four of us run outside and across the big backyard toward the garage, passing the old tire hanging on a tree where sometimes we watch Lenny throw ten, twelve, fifteen perfect football passes through the middle and win twenty dollars each from Jorge and Nick, who bet that he can't do that anymore. We run like children because this energy is very nervous and it is a long time until next Saturday and so we need to play some music.

Inside, I strap on my guitar and we warm up a little, and then everyone wants to hear the new song. Maggie sits down near the workbench and Lenny relaxes at his drums and Nick stands with his guitar on his shoulder, but not playing, just listening and tapping his foot. I sing it once all the way through, just me, and then I go right into singing it again, and this time Nick is nodding his encouragement and joining in with some chords, and now so does Lenny with the drums; Maggie, she is giving us the thumbs-up where she is sitting and listening, and for once just being Maggie, with no flash cards and no schoolbooks. And a few times I am looking back at Lenny (who I can tell is liking this new song), and he is looking at me with his handsome brown eyes, and I think he is asking me with those eyes if after we are finished playing tonight in his garage, maybe I would like to stay awhile.

MAGGIE

This new song, it is very good, too. I am thinking how this must be like they say in my Vo-Tech English class—an "irony." (This was on our last test, and it means something that is the opposite of what you might expect. Our teacher, she says sometimes this irony can be funny or sad or somewhere in the middle.) So I am thinking about the *irony* of the new song about a lost soldier who meets a Gypsy, and how this kind of irony is both funny and sad, depending on who you are. If you are Carmen or Lenny, it is funny because the soldier in the song is the shy cadet, Ryan Sweeney, and because Carmen told me in Marco's car that she said *adiós* to that cadet at Placido's—that she ran out on him and told him they are done, over, good-bye. This is funny because now that song about him is sounding like another hit for the Gypsy Lovers, and it is funny, too, that while Carmen is singing this song for the first time in Lenny's garage, Lenny and Carmen are starting to look at each other like maybe they have given up trying to keep business and pleasure separate. But if you are Ryan Sweeney, this irony is sad because he does not get to keep the beautiful Gypsy girl who is maybe getting a chance at her dream to become a famous singer, and she is getting this chance partly because of songs about him!

When they are finished, we go back inside the house and sit around playing cards and talking and listening to Nick's new CD of Stevie Ray Vaughan. We call Jorge at the airport, where he is working overtime at his security-guard job, but he says he is too busy to talk. Lenny says that's good because everyone should keep their regular jobs in case the music contract doesn't happen. Carmen looks sad and pushes out her lower lip when he says this, and Lenny, he laughs a little and he takes her chin in his big drummer's hand, and he is kissing her on the forehead but not like your grandfather or uncle kisses you on the forehead. And Nick and me, we are looking across the room at each other like maybe we should leave.

At ten-thirty, Nick says to Lenny: "I'm tired, I'm outta here." He says to Carmen, "I'll drive Maggie home," and then over his shoulder as we are walking out: "See you Wednesday for rehearsal at Gallagher's."

In the car, I ask Nick if he is mistaken about the rehearsal on Wednesday being at Gallagher's because that is always their 2-for-1 Happy Hour Night, and where will the band practice their sets if the bar is open?

"Tommie is closing up so we can have the place to ourselves— to get everything right for Saturday when those guys from New York are here."

"How'd you do that? He will lose money, no?"

"It was Carmen's idea," Nick says. "She told Tommie that if the Gypsy Lovers get a recording contract, then we will make sure that any photos of the band include the front of Gallagher's Pub. Of course, Tommie likes the idea of his pub on the cover of CDs and on the Web site of the music company. So he says OK, just this time, just this once. Five to seven o'clock."

I get home around eleven and I am too tired to move the clothes off my bed. I throw my pillow onto the floor and lie down on my rug, and I am just starting to fall asleep when I hear the phone downstairs in the hallway ringing.

"*¡Maldito sea!*" I can hear Mami saying. "Who is calling us so late?" And I am saying a little prayer it is not the police to tell her one of my brothers is in trouble.

I listen now to hear what Mami is saying and then: "Maggie! *¡Vea!* Come here! It's for you!" And so I lift my tired bones off the floor and go to the phone Mami is handing me. With a smile on her lips, she whispers, "It's a boy . . . ," as if this is something she has been looking forward to all her life. I wait for her to go back to the kitchen before I speak.

"This is Maggie. Who is this, please?"

"Oh—uh—good. Maggie. I already called two of the wrong Ruíz numbers. This is Ryan. Ryan Sweeney."

I do not know why Ryan Sweeney is calling me. And I especially do not know why he is calling me (and apparently some of my cousins) at eleven o'clock at night. I sit down on the floor, my back against the wall under the stairs. I hope this doesn't take too long.

RYAN

For the rest of Friday night, I think about the things I obviously did right: Carmen liked that day in Valley Forge Park—so maybe informal dates work better. Maybe she is more at ease that way. Then I think about the things that I screwed up: she didn't like it when I called her cell phone. OK, I can live without that. Maybe she'd be OK with e-mail. She said she didn't own a computer but she used Maggie's.

Maggie. She seems like a nice person. And obviously, she is very close with Carmen. "Since we were babies," Carmen told me that night at Gallagher's, "like sisters, me and Maggie." Looking back, I probably should have gotten to know Maggie Ruíz better. She might have been able to tip me off about what happened tonight. Maybe I could have avoided it altogether.

I lie there for a few hours going back over every minute I spent with Carmen, every conversation, every touch and every kiss, trying to discover the root of what went wrong. After a while, I walk down the hall and get a soda from the machine in the common room. Robbie Clements, the one with the flu, is sprawled out on the couch watching some late-night talk show. I stay there sipping my Mountain Dew and watch as the host introduces the musical guest: some up-and-coming rock band out of Texas. The lights come up, and the lead singer—an attractive redhead in her early twenties, I'd say—steps from the shadows to the microphone and begins to sing. I watch and listen until the song's finished, all the while thinking: *She's pretty and they're good . . . but honestly? Carmen and her band are a lot better.*

And then just that thought—just remembering how Carmen looked and how she sang that night at Gallagher's—makes me go crazy again. My hand shakes around the soda can, my heart pounds inside my chest. My mind, like a malfunctioning jukebox, flips through its obsessive questions: *What if she won't come back to me? (Did I ever really have her?) What if it's really over and she refuses to talk to me? How will I survive without seeing her? Without hearing her voice? Without holding her?*

A new sense of urgency overtakes me. I hurry back to my room and pull down the phone book from the top closet shelf. I flip to the *R*s, then to the *Ru*s: Ruggierro, Ruhalster, Ruíz. Damn! There are several dozen of them. OK—but she lives in Carmen's neighborhood, and Carmen lives somewhere near Valley Forge. I take my highlighter and slide it across the names that have a Valley Forge, Wayne, or St. Davids address. That brings it down to a dozen. OK, here goes. . . .

"No Maggie here, dude." *Click.* That's the first number I try.

The second is an older guy. "Nah, we got no one by that name livin' here—sorry!" At least he was polite.

I dial the third number: Ruíz, E. *"Sí,"* a kind female voice replies when I ask to speak to Maggie Ruíz. *"Momento,* you hold on, OK?" Bingo!

Carmen's best friend answers, sounding tired and a little annoyed. I apologize for calling so late. I take a deep breath and state my case:

"Listen, Maggie. I was wondering if you could do me a favor— see, I think I messed up with Carmen. She's not so happy with me right now, but I need to set things right between us. I know she's kind of—um—strong-willed, but I also know she will listen to you and I thought—um—maybe you could talk to her for me . . . convince her that I'm worth another try, that I'm not a bad guy." I struggle to speak calmly and logically, attempting to hide how desperately I need her help, how crazy and wretched I feel without Carmen.

Maggie sighs wearily. "Carmen does not think you are a bad guy. She never says this to me. And me and Carmen—we talk *a lot*. I think that Carmen just . . . well . . . she just needs to be *Carmen*. And that means being free most of the time for her music, which is her dream—"

"Yeah, I *know*," I interrupt. "You have to tell her for me that I'm cool with the music thing. I just need Carmen to say she's still mine. And even if she spends ninety percent of her time writing and singing and rehearsing, and the other ten percent of her time with me—that I'm cool with that. *I'll take ten percent.* As long as she says we're together. Only us. Her and me. Ryan and Carmen. Together."

There's silence on the other end of the line. "Maggie? Are you there?"

Part 6

A man turns into a villain without realizing what is happening to him.

Prosper Mérimée, CARMEN

MAGGIE

This boy, Ryan, he has got it *bad* for Carmen. He is desperate, like a beggar who has not eaten for a week. Do I feel sorry for him? *Claro*, of course I do. Like I felt sorry for all the other boys who came before him. Maybe more, though, because he is like a dog who is tied too long to the porch and fed only scraps of bread— and then someone comes and offers him good food and sets him free. And then that dog, he is so grateful he is always licking your hand and staying right at your heels, like a shadow.

"Ryan," I say, trying to be as patient as I can. "Let me tell you something about Carmen: she does not belong to anybody. I think you'd better just leave things alone and—"

"No! I won't! I mean—I *can't*. I can't give up. I just—I just can't do that."

(Oh, brother, here we go. This dog is stubborn like a mule.) "But—"

"Look, Maggie," he interrupts again. "I'm going to lay low for the next few days, give her some time to cool off. But then I'm planning to come by the store on Wednesday, late afternoon. . . . I was hoping maybe you could convince Carmen to talk to me and—"

"Carmen has rehearsal on Wednesday," I hear myself say in a not-so-patient voice. (Two can play at this interrupting game! Who does he think I am, his personal assistant? It is almost eleven-thirty at night and I am tired and I am not responsible for fixing this boy's life.) "So you see, I can't do that for you because she will be at Gallagher's getting ready for their gig on Saturday," I explain. "And this is her big chance at her dream, so if you care about her, you can just stay away and let her have her chance, OK?" I slam the phone down and take my tired bones back upstairs. If this is how love is, if this is how crazy you have to be—then maybe I will not get married someday after all. Maybe, instead, I will be an old woman with many cats. Yes. That sounds good to me. No husband and no sons. Just cats. Maybe then I can get some rest.

May 4, 2007

Dear Ryan:

Well, there's good news and bad news. I'll get the bad stuff out of the way first. Three days ago, we were out on foot patrol in the marketplace when a little kid came running up and offered a piece of fruit to Vince Henderson, one of the new guys in the unit. Vince accepted it (we're supposed to be "winning the trust of the locals"), but before any of us could shout a warning, the thing exploded, and there stood Vince with a bloody stump where his right arm should have been. The kid was long gone and perfectly safe, of course. I was just steps away when it happened and I can't stop thinking about it. A kid. An apple. Ten, maybe fifteen, seconds. That's all it took. Boom. No arm. Nothing the same for him ever again. His whole life changed, just like that.

That's the kind of stuff they don't teach you about at the V, little brother. There's no drill for the smiling-kid-giving-you-exploding-fruit. And honestly, Ry, you know, if it had been me—honestly—I think I'd rather die. I lay awake most of last night asking myself if it was really worth it. I know we're not supposed to think this way, but I couldn't help it. I kept looking across my body at my biceps, elbow, forearm, wrist, and hand—always there, ready and able to do pretty much whatever I ask them to. I tried to imagine poor Vince lying across the compound in that hospital bed looking down at his shoulder and seeing . . . nothing. Artificial limbs and full pension be damned.

OK, now for the more cheerful part of this letter. Partly on account of there being more of that kind of thing happening lately (last week, a roadside bomb took out two of our guys in a "bomb-proof" jeep), and partly because another of our new guys used to work concessions at the Second City in Chicago, our unit's formed a comedy improv. We have our second show tonight, and we're all pretty stoked about it. The director, Jared Clark (we call him Windy, for the city, but also 'cause you don't want to sit next to him in a cramped Humvee when he's had seconds on chili), has asked me to do my George W. imitation, so I'm practicing my bad-grammared, good ol' boy, "Shucks—can you believe they voted me in twice?" monologue whenever I can. The first show was a huge success; even our CO, who's a good soldier but rarely cracks a smile, was laughing like a schoolboy at the White House picnic skit featuring three of our guys dressed as Hillary Clinton, Condoleezza Rice, and Laura Bush.

In fact, I gotta memorize the end of my script this afternoon, so I'll sign off now and do that. I imagine you're pretty busy with classes and with your new girl (photos are always welcome, little bro—not much eye candy over here), but getting news from you or from Mom cheers me up for weeks, so even if it's a short letter or e-mail, you knucklehead, write!

Yours in tragedy and comedy,
Adam

WILL

My alarm goes off at seven. I roll over, bang it silent. Across the room, Ry's bed is already made and he's standing by the closet, pulling on running shoes and shorts. I stumble out of the sheets, grab a towel and some soap.

"We beat the G Company plebes," I tell him before I head to the showers. "Sixty-four to fifty-one."

Ryan nods and high-fives me halfheartedly. The old Ryan would've relished such a victory against our rival company, a group of guys whose athletic talent is matched only by their confidence. But the new Ryan appears unimpressed.

"So—how was the big restaurant date?" I ask, changing the subject.

Ryan squats to retie an already perfectly tied running shoe. "Fine," he mumbles to the floor. "Nice place."

Hmmm. This doesn't sound like the post-Carmen euphoria I'm used to.

"I'm going for a run. Probably won't be back for a while. . . ." Ryan's voice fades away like one of those old country-music songs, the ones where the artist was too lazy (or too drunk) to write a real ending. I watch him jog to the opposite end of the hall and push open the door to the stairs, his shoulders slumped like someone who's been beaten. I don't need a PhD in psychology to tell me there's trouble in Ryan Sweeney's paradise.

As for me, the rest of Saturday morning isn't exactly paradise—but it's not bad, either: shower, breakfast, KP duty, then over to the library to start that philosophy paper. At noon, it's back to the mess hall to eat lunch and collect payments for cigarette orders. (I can't prove it, but there's a good chance that the phrase "under the table" originated in a military school.) A few quick games of foosball in the rec hall afterward, then over to the garage, where Sergeant O'Connor leans against the side of the supply truck, grinning widely.

"Martens! I was wondering if you'd show." He spreads his arms out before him, a king surveying his vast territory. "Today's my birthday and I'm feeling lucky, so we're definitely stopping for some coffee and lottery tickets . . . and maybe you'll even get a chance to hit on that lovely counter girl I told you about."

"Yes sir! And happy birthday, sir," I reply with as much sincerity as I can muster.

A few minutes later, we pass through the front gate and head down the road into town. In the distance, across the empty athletic fields, I glimpse a small figure running up and down the steep hillside that separates the track from the soccer field. Arms pumping, legs churning beneath him, he runs like someone possessed.

CARMEN

"Mike the driver, he is moving back to New York so his sister can help out with the kids," I tell the blond cadet when he comes to pick up his cigarettes. He takes this news pretty good, too. He says it is already May, so in a few weeks almost everyone at VFMA will be leaving for the summer anyway.

I am taking my afternoon break, and Will is talking to me out front after putting the box with the cigarettes in the back of the big green army truck. Through the store window, we can see the happy sergeant picking his Powerball numbers and telling old soldier stories to Fat Frank, who is listening and laughing and rubbing his belly.

"So . . . ," I say between sips of my Dr Pepper. "Did Ryan tell you we are through?" I offer him my soda.

"Not in so many words. But it wasn't too hard to figure out that something bad happened last night between you two," Will says. He takes a sip and hands the bottle back to me. "Ry really likes you, you know. Even though he's been a pain in the ass to be around since you guys started hanging out together—he does really, really like you."

"I know that. But he is too . . . too . . . he is too much like this,

you know?" I tell him, putting my hands to my throat like someone is choking me.

"Carmen—break's over!" Fat Frank yells through the door
he has opened just a little, but enough so I can see the sergeant
walking toward the counter with his coffee and sandwich and his
Powerball card.

"It was great doing business with you, Carmen," Will says, extending his right hand. "Maybe we can set up something again
when I'm back on campus next year."

"*Buena suerte.* Good luck!" I say, shaking his hand and
tossing my empty bottle into the trash.

I go back inside and start the second half of my shift. The
soccer mommies are arriving now with their cleated sons and
daughters, and the lawyers with the nice watches who play tennis are coming in for herbal iced tea. I smile politely and count
out their change, but also I pray silently: *Please, Mother Mary, full
of grace . . . let my voice be strong on Saturday, let me not be
behind this counter when the cadets come back next year.*

MAGGIE

And OK, so *most* of the time I am not feeling jealous of Carmen and the way men are always looking at her, like she is a cool glass of water and they have been walking for days through the parched desert, crazy with thirst. Most of the time, no, this does not bother me. But just once in a while (and I never know when this will happen—it is like the one-day flu: it comes, then just as quick, it goes), I am wondering, imagining . . . and yes, I am even dreaming . . . what it would be like to trade places with my best friend, my beautiful *hermana*. On those days, I picture myself walking through the King of Prussia Mall, my hips swinging, my hair falling dark and silky on my back, my smooth skin and red-lipped smile sending out silent signals to all the males in those corridors so that they—innocent and unknowing—must turn their heads toward me and stare, wide-eyed and unbelieving, at this amazing creature, this girl who appears to be human, like them, but then again, she is so perfect and so appealing, how could she be one of their own species? And then (they cannot help themselves, I know—you can see it in their eyes, every time) they cannot stop looking, and if they are walking one way, a quick pivot—ha!—and see how easy to be going now the opposite way and so much better the chance that they might even pass by and look closer at that face and into those eyes that are deep and green like the sea.

So.

This happens. Sometimes. Not often. Not for very long. Like I said, it comes, it goes. I shake myself. I go into the bathroom and close the door. I face the mirror on the wall and take a long look. Maggie Ruíz. I am still this person. Still this Maggie of the plain face, the not-very-smooth skin, the small hips and flat chest. I am not Carmen Navarro, who makes the boys crazy with desire. No.

But . . . I am her sister, Carmen's *hermana*. And I am plain, not ugly. No. Not that.

And I am smart when I am working hard to be smart. And I am loyal. I am like a pair of good, solid shoes that you know will carry you many miles in comfort and not wear out.

And these things that I am, they are all good. They all add up to a life, a good life. They are enough.

WILL

Back on campus, it takes me less than thirty minutes to make my deliveries. I stuff the cigarettes into one of the clean-laundry bags, which makes them easy to carry inconspicuously across campus to the dorm. While I'm at it, I deliver the clean shirts and pants, too—no extra charge!

I'm about ten paces from our room when I slow down a little, my personal radar focused on the small piece of paper tacked on the door at eye level. Ever since I've been here, no one has left us a note—we're fined and punished if we "defile, degrade, or otherwise destroy" VFMA property. I can already imagine the extra KP duty we'll be doing for the pin-size hole in the wood. I step close enough to read the neatly printed lines:

> *Ryan,*
> *Meet me at the library as soon as you get back. I'll be*
> *waiting.*

The note is unsigned. But I can tell by the way the letters line up perfectly, almost like they were typed, the way the marker is pressed heavily into the paper and the tack's driven into the door,

I can tell you exactly who wrote it. And knowing Colonel Sweeney as I do, I also know he didn't drive up to campus just to say hi, just to have a friendly chat and take Ryan out for ice cream. No sir. That's not Colonel Sweeney's style. And even though I've been pretty pissed at Ryan lately, even though there've been plenty of times in the past that I wished I *had* a father (who, at least, I knew and could talk to, even if he was a too-strict son of a gun), as I look closely at this note—especially the way *I'll be waiting* is almost engraved into the page—well, this is one time I'm glad I'm *not* my roommate.

RYAN

We sit across from each other at a table in the library archives, surrounded by commissioned portraits of every distinguished graduate since the school opened. In this bastion of military history, this altar of achievement, self-sacrifice, and discipline, my father makes it perfectly clear that I am failing him, failing the family, failing the Academy, failing the freakin' *country*, with my wild and immature behavior. This, of course, is not news to me. Even his surprise visit here today really isn't surprising. . . . He and the general go way back and have kept in close touch since they were cadets. I guess I knew it was only a matter of time until he arrived at VFMA to chew me out.

"I'm not sure what's gotten into you, son, but whatever it is—drugs, booze, or just plain sloth—you damn well better quit!" He waves the typed letter from Major Adare, addressed to him, about an inch from my face. I got my own copy a few days ago, on the dean's personal letterhead—not in my campus mailbox, but delivered by a plebe who came directly to my room. The letter said I was in danger of failing, and that if things continued, I would not be asked back to the Academy. I had read it, all right, but then it went straight to the trash. At the time, I had much more pleasant things to think about, including my Friday-night date with Carmen.

"Ryan . . ." My father is trying mightily to hold his temper in check. But the color in his face and the veins popping out on his neck testify to the depth of his anger. "Ryan, do you realize that you were on the fast track to West Point? Do you realize that your brother is fighting bravely over there in that godforsaken desert where people blow themselves up every half hour and you . . . you are here without a care in the world, squandering your future and acting like some spoiled two-year-old?!"

I sit there, not saying anything, my expression as blank as I can make it. The truth is, I knew this day would come. . . . I knew, even as I crept back into the dorm after that first night with Carmen at Gallagher's, that I was subverting everything my family stood for, everything I'd been taught to believe in: loyalty to my corps, loyalty to the Academy, pride in my achievements. I'd been taught to work hard and make sacrifices in the present in return for a future of security, status, and respect.

But starting that night, I gave away all of that for a beautiful, raven-haired high school dropout who dreams of being a pop star and who, as it turns out, doesn't return my loyalty and affection. Despite the sane advice from my roommate, the loss of respect from my corps, my failing grades, and even the red-flag warnings occasionally sent up from the more logical, intellectual parts of my own brain—despite *all* of that, Carmen somehow possessed me. With that first flirtatious look, with that first long-stemmed gift, and with that first amazing kiss, the Gypsy girl vanquished all my reason and discipline.

Now here I am at the crossroads. In giving my heart and soul to Carmen, I have split myself in two. I am a house divided, a house that will fall in upon itself unless I choose which half can stay, and which half must go. As I sit at this table across from my father, the two Ryans are engaged in a great struggle. The old Ryan wants to win back his father's respect, to win back the general's respect, to win back his best friend's respect. The old Ryan wants to put recent events behind him and move forward, to do whatever it will take to get into West Point and become an officer.

But the new Ryan wants no part of that. The new Ryan wants to strip off the uniform and run out the front gate as fast as his legs will carry him; wants to lose himself in the crowds at the mall; wants to dress in cutoffs, dirty sneakers, and a T-shirt; wants to find Carmen and stare into her deep green eyes and touch her smooth olive skin and tell her he is hers, only hers, and that he is through with the Academy, through with generals and rules and schedules, through with the terrible burden of his family's honor and reputation. The new Ryan imagines her kissing him deeply. He imagines taking her hand and running for the bus that will take them to the station in Philadelphia, where they will buy a pair of one-way tickets to Canada or Mexico and never look back.

"Ryan . . . *Ryan!*" My father's voice breaks into my dream. The film reel snaps. The beautiful love story ends—the spell is broken. Thinking clearly now, I understand that it's only in my dreams that she belongs to me. In reality, she doesn't love me. She doesn't think of me when we're apart. I am—I have been—living a desperate, self-destructive dream.

As the realization sinks in, I feel a strange combination of pain and relief. The new Ryan falls silent; when I answer my father, the old Ryan speaks: "Dad, look—I know I've slipped. I know I've disappointed you and Mom. I know I've let down my men and the Academy. I wish I could explain it to you, but . . . I can't. But, Dad . . ." I reach over and touch his hand, something I've never done before, even as a little boy. My voice becomes stronger, more serious now. "You have my word that things are going to get better. I'm going to start now to put things right. I'm going to make up all my missed class work. I'm going to raise my grades. I'm going to be the neatest, shiniest cadet on the whole campus at every inspection. I'm going to show up early and stay late for all my duties. Heck, I'll even stay for the summer session if I have to. . . ."

My father's eyes narrow as he listens to my list of promises. I guess I can't blame him for being skeptical. Still, his shoulders relax a bit, and I can see that he wants to believe me, wants to walk over to his old pal General Hirshman's office and reassure him that everything's going to be all right.

I stand and extend my right hand. He rises and shakes my hand, and we part as we always do, with an abrupt snap-down military salute.

MAGGIE

On Tuesday after Vo-Tech, I meet Carmen at the mall and we shop for the lucky outfit she will wear at Gallagher's on Saturday. Carmen says after she pays off those two new chairs and some heart medicines for her *abuelos*, after the electric bill and her part of the postage for shipping those CDs and photos up to the music studio, she has exactly seventy dollars left. I tell her don't worry, we'll find something.

We go into every department store and most of the ladies' boutiques and still we can find nothing that fits or looks just right. At eight o'clock our feet are tired and our stomachs growl with hunger. We go to the food court and get a large order of french fries and two Cokes, and we sit and eat at a wobbly table with mustard stains and KAYLA LOVES BRENDAN carved into the corner.

"You know, maybe it's better if I wear my red and black outfit, because it is comfortable and anyway that is one less thing to worry about when I am looking out into the crowd and seeing those two guys from the studio and I am feeling so nervous I am shaking in my shoes. Maybe it is meant to be like this, Maggie, you think?"

I rip open the last packet of ketchup and drizzle it across the top of my last little pile of fries. "You look great in your red and black outfit," I reply, stuffing the french fries one by one into my mouth and washing them down with my soda. I look around for a trash can and that is when I see a lady in the window of Mimi Jon's Boutique dressing a mannequin in a short sleeveless dress that is shimmery gold like the top of Marco's wrestling trophies.

"That one there—see?" I say, pointing behind Carmen to where the woman is zipping up the back and adding a pair of gold sandals to the mannequin's feet. "That is the dress you must get."

We toss our trash and walk over to the shop, where Carmen points to the gold dress and mouths to the saleslady, *How much?*

The lady turns over the tag hanging from the armpit so we can see the numbers that tell Carmen she is ninety dollars short.

"*¡Ay Señor!* I drank too much soda!" I tell Carmen, holding my guts and rolling my eyes. "I'm going to the restroom. You go inside there and see if maybe you can find something else you like. I'll be right back."

I don't give my friend time to argue. I watch her walk into the store and begin to look at the other dresses on the racks, and then I walk down the hallway toward the sign that says RESTROOMS next to the sign that says INFORMATION and ATM. I slip my bank card into the little slot and put in my pass code. I touch the screen for ACCOUNT BALANCE, and for just a few seconds, I savor the miracle that is the two with the three zeros following behind. I touch WITHDRAWAL and punch in $100. I press ENTER, and the five crisp twenty-dollar bills appear in the slot at the bottom. I push NO, that I don't want another transaction, and get my card back. I count the bills. I smell them. I push them deep into my pocket. That was the easy part. Now I must convince Carmen to take them and buy that dress.

WILL

I haven't asked Ry about his dad's visit, and he hasn't mentioned it, either. He still seems preoccupied and jumpy. And yet, *something* must've happened between him and his old man, because now there are glimpses of the rule-driven, ultra-responsible Cadet Captain Ryan Sweeney. Like on Monday after first mess. We're heading to class when he asks if I've finished my philosophy paper. "Yeah. It's pretty lame, though. I'm hoping for a C-minus," I tell him. "You do yours yet? It's due this afternoon, you know."

Ryan reaches into his satchel and pulls out a neatly typed document. "Spent most of last night finishing it."

I read the title page: *"Beauty: What's Behind the Eyes of the Beholder."* "Sounds like some good reading," I say sarcastically.

"Not really," Ryan says, replacing the paper carefully. "But Major Breyer will eat it up. It's exactly the kind of rambling, high-falutin crap he loves."

We're almost at the end of the quad, where we have to split up and head separately to our eight a.m. classes. "You got your Breyer assignment with you?" Ryan asks.

"It's back in the room. I was gonna stop by and get it after second mess. . . . Why?"

Ryan shrugs. "My ten o'clock's canceled, so I'm free for two hours after this class. I could, you know, read over your paper and edit it a little . . . maybe even bring you up to a C!" He fake-punches me on the arm, grinning. Now *this* is more like the Ryan I grew up with.

"Sure!" I say. "It's still in the printer. Help yourself. Just leave it there when you're done and I'll make the changes after second mess. . . . Thanks, man."

That was Monday. But on Tuesday, he was back to his weirdness. When I came into our room after second mess, I found him leaning over his little wastebasket, burning a photograph of himself and his father that was taken during our first plebe week.

He seemed not to notice me, so I cleared my throat to let him know I was back.

"Hey," he said, looking up suddenly. His face appeared drawn and sad, his expression confused. "Sorry I missed lunch."

"What are you doing?" I asked when he didn't offer an explanation as to why he had an open flame going a few inches from his bed. I could just imagine the instant apoplexy if one of the adult officers happened by in the hall. I quickly closed the door.

Ryan turned back to the photo, watching the edges curl and the image of the two faces—his own and his father's—melt into a thin glue. "I'm just getting rid of some old stuff . . . ," he said, reaching for another photo behind him and holding it over the center of the can.

I stepped closer. This picture was smaller: four by six inches or less. I squinted, trying to make out the image, which wasn't a close-up. I took another step. "Careful!" Ryan warned me. "I'm not interested in scorching any innocents here. . . ." I looked at the photo again just as the edges caught fire: it was Carmen, standing next to the large painted sign at the main entrance of Valley Forge Park. Ry had taken it with his phone and later made a print of it for his desk. The image burned quickly.

That was yesterday afternoon, and by evening, the old Ryan seemed to have returned. He hung around with us and laughed a few times at my jokes. After mess, he rejoined our basketball team as we took on K Company. He was a little rusty, but by the end of the second half, he was getting back into the rhythm of full-court hoops. We won by thirteen points, earning a play-off spot in next week's campus championships.

Today, we get our papers back in philosophy. And thanks to my roommate's editing, I get a B-plus, the best I've done in that class all year. Ryan gets what the old Ryan *usually* got—a solid A, with all kinds of ecstatic comments written in red pen in the margins.

After class, we high-five the bronze Eisenhower statue as we make our way down the stairs and outside to the quad, where the afternoon sun beats down on our uniforms. We head to the dorm to throw on our shorts and enjoy some free time before this evening's mandatory study hours.

"You wanna head to the gym, or over to the rec hall, or . . ." I lean out the window and look down at the macadam courts. "It looks like the outside court's open. We could shoot around there and then go to—"

"I gotta make a run into town, Will," Ryan informs me in a flat, matter-of-fact voice, like you'd tell someone you had to take a leak or make a phone call. "And I gotta go alone."

An awkward silence falls over the room. I try to read my friend's expression, but there's not much there to read. I'm unsure about which Ryan this is: the one I've always known, or the weird one that fistfights while on guard duty and burns photos in his room.

"You seeing—uh—*her*?" I ask, a little amazed at my nerve.

Ryan nods. "Yeah, but it's not like you imagine. We . . . we had a falling-out last Friday at the restaurant and since then—I've done some thinking. . . ." His voice trails off. He runs his hand up and down his throat as if he's pushing his voice back up into his mouth. Then he sits down on his bed, whips out his penknife, and starts making small slashes in the sole of his shoe. He concentrates hard on what he's doing, making each small incision exactly like the one beside it. (So—the weirdness has returned.)

"I just need to see her again one last time," he explains, still slashing his shoe and still avoiding my gaze. "If I can do that—if I can walk away on my own terms—then I'll know it's really over. Then I can just get on with things, you know?"

I nod, not because I understand what it's like to be so taken with someone that I temporarily lose my sense of reality, but because we've been best friends since third grade.

And really, when you think about it, what other choice do I have?

RYAN

In the past forty-eight hours, I've made some progress toward picking up the pieces of my life. I've met with my philosophy and history teachers and made up three assignments. Even so, that might not be enough. They both made it pretty clear that depending on how I do in the next couple of weeks, I may have to take some courses this summer. I also scheduled a Friday appointment with Major Adare, to tell him I'm committed to doing whatever it takes to raise my grades and graduate next year near the top of my class. I rejoined our basketball team and played in a semifinal game (we won, thank God—despite my numerous fouls and my lame shooting percentage). I even helped Will on his philosophy paper, which I think he really appreciated.

So—that part has gone well. It's keeping *her* out of my mind that's not been so easy. Every time I hear a female voice on the radio, every time I pass the front gate and see a dark-haired girl on the bus, every time I use my cell phone—in fact, every time I do almost *anything*, I think of Carmen. And if I let myself think of her long enough . . .

I start losing it. I start not caring about anything but her again. I start to ignore my work, my duties, my friends.

It doesn't help that Baji still comes around, either. On Monday morning, as I left the dorm, she was there by the oak tree, her tail swishing, her eyes watching me as I walked across the quad to class. Then the entire period, while Colonel Winberry reviewed for the trigonometry final, I had to wrestle my attention away from memories of our afternoon in Valley Forge Park, the sound of her laugh as she leaped from rock to rock, the smell of her skin when I held her. I had to literally shake myself several times during class, just to stop thinking about it. (I told the guy sitting next to me that I was sleep-deprived, up late finishing a term paper. I'm not sure he was convinced.)

Yesterday I decided to destroy any tangible reminder I had of our time together. Will walked in just as I was about to burn the one good photo I had of her. I knew it wouldn't be easy, so I burned one of my old man first. That went pretty well. Not too hard. Then I lit the corner of Carmen's photograph, and right away, I felt physically ill—like I had just thrown my own body into the flames, too. Afterward, extinguishing the fire and staring down at the scorched place at the bottom of the waste-basket, I felt an odd sense of peace. Something inside me clicked into place again, and for the rest of the evening, I felt like my former self.

Now it's Wednesday and there's just one more thing I need to do: I need to see Carmen again. I need to tell her I'm over her. I need to prove that I'm stronger than any power she has over me. I need to show her (hell, I need to show *myself*) that I'm in charge of my own life again—that I've moved on.

Will takes it pretty well when I explain where I'm going and why. As he leaves to play basketball with the other guys, I change into my khakis and a clean white shirt and try to decide which eager-to-please fourth classman I'll get to sign out with me. But then—no. I want to leave campus alone, one last act of rebellion.

I go out the back of our dorm and walk along the hedgerow next to the fence, until I reach the gate where the landscapers bring in their equipment from the storage shed. No one's around. I stand close to the gate and reach up to grab the post. I pull myself over the top, dropping down with a soft *thud* on the opposite side. Turning south, I walk through the woods toward town.

CARMEN

So I ask Fat Frank if maybe I can leave a little early and go home, get cleaned up, and rest my voice before rehearsal. But of course, Frank is in no mood to hear this. He is scratching his belly and telling me too bad and here, take these trays of soft pretzels and make sure they each get bagged and put in the baskets near the register for the after-work customers.

Maggie, she comes over to help me when there is no one at the deli, but this only lasts until the receptionist from across the street comes in and wants three Italians and two ham and cheeses, and there goes my one chance of leaving early.

So to pass the time between three and four o'clock, when I can finally get out of here, I go over in my head the order of the songs in each set and also some of the lyrics of the new ones so I don't forget when I get nervous on Saturday, which I know I will. I am smiling at the lady who is buying the five hoagies for the dentist's office and counting out her change, and at the same time, I am trying to remember if Lenny said we should sing the refrain for the new song two or three times before the last verse, and thank you, have a nice day, lady with the five hoagies.

At three-thirty, the store is empty and Fat Frank yells from the office for me to take out the trash. I dump the containers from under the counter and also the one from in front of the deli, and then I drag the large plastic bag across the floor and out the side door into the bright sun and street noise. I hum the refrain for the fifth song as I place the bag inside the Dumpster that is just across the parking lot by the fence. And then . . .

Sure, why not?—there is no reason to hurry back inside—I lean against this fence and stretch my legs out in front of me. I close my eyes and feel the sun on my face and neck; I listen to the birds in the trees and the cars passing by on the road. I dream I am wearing the new gold dress that Maggie helped me pay for at the mall, and I am singing with the Gypsy Lovers on a stage somewhere near the ocean, and yes, this is a beautiful dream.

When I open my eyes, here comes a surprise walking toward me.

"Hey!" I call out to Lenny, wiping my hands on my jeans. "What are you doing here?"

"I came by to see if you needed a ride to the pub," Lenny says, looking handsome in his dark jeans and loose white shirt. And of course, this is why he is here—Lenny is always thinking ahead and he is always taking care of me.

"I'm not done yet. Twenty-five more minutes—you want to wait?"

"Yeah, sure," he says. And then he smiles and reaches out to touch my face and to run his fingers across my cheek. "Absolutely, I'll wait."

And now he is looking through me with those brown eyes, and

I am holding his wrist and moving us away from the window so
Fat Frank cannot see. We steal a kiss that tastes like milk and
honey in the warm sunshine on the side of the building, and I
know as long as Lenny is with me on that stage on Saturday, I will
sing like an angel.

RYAN

I didn't ask Maggie what time Carmen's band is rehearsing at Gallagher's. No big deal, though: I have to pass the Quikmart on the way to town, so if she's still working, I can save myself some time. Plus, considering my goal of putting all this behind me, it's probably better to go back to the place where it all started, the place where I first came under Carmen's spell.

Since early this morning, I've been mentally rehearsing the final scene between us: I approach. She sees me, feels a pang of guilt and remorse. I greet her politely, coolly, extending my hand for her to shake. I tell her I've moved on, too—that I'm looking forward to summer, to seeing some of my old friends again. I wish her good luck with her band and with her future. I turn and leave; I feel relieved, released, back in control.

I go over it all once more in my head as I reach the corner. I feel confident, composed. My watch says 3:30. I wait for the traffic light to change before crossing the street, then head down the next block toward the convenience store.

I'm about thirty yards away when I see her leaving the building, dragging a bag of trash across the parking lot. She's wearing the same shirt she wore on the first day I saw her—the one with

THE GYPSY LOVERS written across her chest. Even from here, she looks so sexy, so full of life. I tell myself to keep walking forward (*C'mon, Ryan, you can do this, you* must *do this. . . .*), but my body isn't listening. All of a sudden, it's like I'm walking into a strong headwind. I slow down, then before too long—it's no use—I stop.

I slip behind the hedge next to the sidewalk and watch as she deposits the plastic bag. She starts back toward the store, then suddenly reconsiders and turns around. She leans against the wooden fence, her face tilted toward the sun. (My God, was she that beautiful before? Yes, of course she was. That's exactly how she looked the day we spent together at Valley Forge Park. The day I felt like I'd never felt before with a girl. The day I had to stop myself from running after her bus as it pulled away.) Now, looking at her stretched out in the sun in the parking lot of the store where she first slipped me that red rose, I feel exactly that way: the familiar rush of blood to my head, the sudden throbbing in my chest, as if whatever's in there can't be contained by bones and skin. I open and close my hands; my palms sweat. Did I really think I could do this? Did I really believe I could give her up?

I try to recall the scene I've been imagining—the one I've played and replayed—the one where I am cool and calm and unfeeling as we exchange a few polite words, grasp hands, and go off into our separate lives. I shake my head. How could I have thought that was possible? Well . . . it's *not* possible. I stand there, looking at her, wanting her more now than I ever have. I know only one thing for certain: I must have her back. I must convince her—right now—that we belong together.

Cautiously I step out from behind the bushes, not knowing

what I will say or how I will act, just allowing myself to be pulled back into her power, a force like no other I've ever known. I concentrate on breathing as I start walking again, my eyes never leaving her.

But . . . wait. Someone is walking toward her from the other direction. I recognize him from . . . yeah, the drummer. Lenny, she calls him. Lenny the drummer, who manages the band. Lenny, who is the oldest member, who has the garage where they practice sometimes, who burns all their CDs and sends them off to studios. I stop walking. He's approaching her. He's . . . *shit!* . . . he's touching her. And she's . . . she's leading him farther back . . . and now they're, now they're—!

Something inside me comes unhinged. I feel it slip as I stand there in the warm sun, watching the girl I thought I could walk away from, the girl I thought I could forget—yes, I realize it now, the girl I *must* have for my own—in someone else's arms.

Strangely, though, I feel none of the panic I felt a few seconds ago. I feel calm. I feel what soldiers must feel just before they head into battle.

MAGGIE

My feet are sore from standing all afternoon behind the deli counter in the new shoes I bought for twelve dollars at Kmart. "They are cute but they will put blisters on your heels, Maggie," Carmen tells me when I show them to her. And of course, my feet are telling me what I should know by now: Carmen is always seeing clear into the future.

Lenny, he comes to the store today, and now I am really feeling like I should disappear whenever he and Carmen are looking that certain way at each other. He gives Carmen and me a ride back to our street and then to Gallagher's, where Tommie the manager has already put up the sign: CLOSED 5 PM–7 PM. TODAY ONLY. Jorge has to work security at the airport till four-thirty, so while Lenny and Nick set up the equipment, Carmen goes over her lyrics and tunes her guitar, and when she is done with that, they are still moving things around and waiting for Jorge and also the new sound-and-lights guy to show up.

"You want me to help you with this homework?" she asks.

"No thanks," I tell her. "See this here?" I hold up my biology book. "I have to study this whole chapter on cancer, and this is not really something you should be thinking about before you sing."

I start to read about pigmentation and mutation and lots of other -*ations* while Carmen pulls out a deck of cards, shuffles a few times, then turns them facedown on the table. She picks three and puts the rest away. (She knows I cannot resist a fortune-telling. I put my textbook down to see what the Fates have in store for her tonight.)

But then I think: *Wait.* I reach across the table and grab her hand before she can turn the first card over.

"Maybe this is not something you should do now," I suggest. "Maybe you should just forget about what the cards say until after Saturday night."

Carmen looks at me like I just said *maybe you should go jump off a bridge.* "I am not afraid of what the cards might say. So what if it is bad? So what if it's good?" She shrugs. "We are all going to live our lives anyhow, right? So let's have a little fun. . . ."

I let go of her wrist. " '*Tá bien,*" I say. "Suit yourself."

First card: the jack of hearts. Second card: the queen of hearts. Third card: the jack of spades.

A matched pair and a third—a rival. I look at Carmen's face, which shows no expression. (Of course, she does not need the cards to tell her this!) But what does it mean to have chosen these cards now?

WILL

We're beating C Company 32–27 on the outside courts. It's just
the first half of a pickup game, but everybody's playing hard, like
it counts. The sun's glare off the gym windows is murder, and the
sweat's pouring in little rivers down my forehead. Curtis, talented
but impulsive, picks up his third foul and sends Robertson to the
free-throw line. I'm shoulder to shoulder with the others, waiting for Robertson's first attempt, when I notice someone who
looks a lot like Ryan walking fast along the far side of the quad.
(But that couldn't be Ryan, could it? He said he was going into
town to see Carmen "one last time." I figured that'd take him an
hour, at least.)

   I turn my attention back to the game. Robertson makes the
first free throw, misses the second. I grab the rebound. I pass it
down the court to McCormick, who's making a break for our bas-
ket. He pulls up, shoots a jumper from the top of the key. *Swoosh!*
God, I do love this game. Our team is really playing well today, but
C Company is, too. Plus, they're all a few inches taller than we are.
Now I'm hoping that *was* Ryan I saw over there and that he's
heading up to the room to change. We could really use his help on
defense in the second half.

RYAN

Lenny goes back to his car and Carmen goes back to work. Right then, I decide not to approach her in the store. No. Much better to wait until the whole band is at Gallagher's. Better that she's occupied with something she loves to do. Yes. Much better. Much. Plus . . . I need some time to get ready. To prepare. To think.

I call the pub on my cell, ask if they're open regular hours tonight. "After seven—we're closed for a private event from five to seven," the voice on the other end says, and hangs up. That was easy enough. Now I know they'll start playing around five. I have some time.

I start walking back to campus. I'd brought along just my phone and ten bucks, but now I need to gather everything I have—the stash of twenties from under my desk drawer, my ATM card, my license and credit cards. I have plenty of time to do that and still get to Gallagher's for the beginning of their rehearsal. Plenty of time.

Heading back to the dorm, I consider stopping by the courts to say good-bye to Will. But everyone else will be there, too—and then I'll have to explain why I'm not in the game and where I'm going. (Where *am* I going? I don't know . . . I don't really care.

As long as she's with me. We'll just take a taxi into the city and we'll get on a train. We'll have time to talk. We'll figure the rest out later.) So—it's better this way. I'll contact Will in a couple of days, from wherever Carmen and I end up.

God, just the thought of that . . . me and Carmen—away—together—the idea of that makes my heart leap. I don't know how I'm going to do it. But I know I *will* do it. I know my very existence depends on it. I can't live without her. I know that now. My father could visit me and lecture me a hundred more times and the result would be the same: I cannot live without her. Can*not*. And she will see this, I'm sure. She'll see it and realize that she should be with me, Ryan Sweeney, the one who would do anything . . . *anything* for her. Who needs her like he needs air. Yes, I'm certain. She will see that clearly. She will come with me. Tonight. Forever.

CARMEN

At five-fifteen, the sound-and-lights guy is finally here, and then Jorge comes in cursing the traffic on the Schuylkill Expressway. He is still wearing his security-guard uniform and his holster, and we laugh because the sight of him bursting through the back door into the big room is like a badly made Western movie. He is still cursing the traffic as he unfastens his holster and pulls off his uniform shirt and throws them onto a table against the wall near the center of the room.

I leave Maggie to her studying and follow him up to the stage. We do a few sound checks for the new guy, who Lenny said is more expensive but also more experienced and will help us look and sound our best. We adjust the amps and the mikes and warm up a little before we begin. The first song is a little rough—not enough bass and too fast on the chorus—but then the second and third songs are sounding much better. My voice is relaxed and the guys are playing really focused, like this is already Saturday, when everything needs to be perfect.

The lights dim. I take a quick drink of water and we begin the fourth song, which is our new one about the lost soldier trying to find his way home. We are just starting the refrain when Baji appears out of nowhere and scampers (very fast, like her tail is on fire) straight across the stage. I don't know why this surprises me because Baji is always appearing out of nowhere, but this time even I am flinching a little, and I feel the hair on the back of my neck stand up.

I keep singing. I look over at Lenny, who is nodding to me to just keep going. (And of course Lenny is right, because who knows what crazy thing might happen in the crowd on Saturday night, when those guys from New York are here and we are trying to win a contract?) I sing the refrain and then the second and the third verses. Lenny nails the drum solo and then we sing the refrain again:

> *Oh, he's traveled so far, so far, so far*
> *He's wandered so long, so long, so long*
> *And he wants to go home, go home, go home.*
> *Please bring him back home,*
> *Please bring him back home.*

I take a few deep breaths when we are done and the lights go all the way down. I can hear clapping out there somewhere in the big open room and I smile to myself, because Maggie is our best fan and she never lets me down. I take another sip of water, and when I turn around again, I see someone (*¡coño!* this is not Maggie who is clapping!) walking toward the stage. He stops his applause but he keeps walking, and now he comes close enough so I can see his face.

The cards never lie, the Gypsies say. I put the microphone back on the stand. I walk forward to meet him.

MAGGIE

Right after Carmen finishes the new song, I see something move in the middle of the darkened room. I don't see it clearly, but I have been around Carmen long enough to read the signs: Baji streaks across the stage like a rabbit being chased by wolves; the cards that Carmen chose only minutes ago show a matched pair and a rival.

So.

I still don't see his face, but of course, I am pretty sure this shadow person is Ryan Sweeney. He hasn't seen me, though. He must have come in through the back door. He was clapping after the song, but now he is standing in the middle of the room with his arms folded over his chest and staring straight at Carmen, and she is walking away from the stage to meet him. All along, I have been afraid there might be trouble from this boy who is so crazy for her. Yes, crazy. "Madly in love," people say . . . and there is good reason why they choose these words.

"Nice song," Ryan says to her in a gruff voice. "That's a new one, huh?"

"Yeah, it's new," Carmen replies. Her voice is flat and has no feeling. Will there be trouble? Ryan Sweeney is a cadet, but he is,

I think, also a boy who is desperate for Carmen's affection. How far will he go?

The room, which was filled with sound only seconds ago, grows suddenly silent. On the stage behind Carmen, Nick and Jorge put down their instruments, and Lenny stands up behind the drums.

Slowly the sound guy brings up the lights.

RYAN

Carmen keeps walking until she is about three paces in front of me. She stops, puts her hands on her hips. "What do you want?" she asks.

She looks so sexy, so alive, standing there, her defiance just increasing my attraction.

After a few seconds, I hear myself reply, in a voice I don't quite recognize as my own. "What do I *want*?" I laugh, and this seems to startle her. "Are you really asking me what I *want*?" She smells delicious—a mixture of roses and smoke. I must have her.

"I want *you*," I tell her in a half-whispered voice. "Can't you see that it has to be this way? I'll do anything for you, Carmen. Anything at all. . . . Come with me and you'll see . . . you'll see we are supposed to be together." I glance over her shoulder at Lenny, who is standing behind the drums. "No one loves you like I do. *No one.*"

I wait for her to say something back to me. She doesn't. Instead, she glares at me with those huge green eyes as if I am the enemy. She is steel, she is ice.

"You are crazy, Red," she says finally, her voice steady and matter-of-fact. Then, leaning toward me and through clenched teeth: "I told you at Placido's that we are through. I will tell you again now: *¡Hemos terminado!* That's it. We're finished. You go back now to your soldier school and leave me alone!"

She pivots on one foot and, tossing her thick black mane off her shoulder, begins to walk away.

I shiver. With each step she takes, I feel more panicked. I'd thought I could at least coax her away from the group—maybe into the back room, where I could make her see—but she's not even going to listen to me. My eyes scan the room, assessing my options. They land on an amazing gift—perhaps the only thing that can save me. I move quickly to grab it.

MAGGIE

The cards never lie. This is what Carmen is always telling me, and of course being half Gypsy, she knows these things. Tonight the cards revealed a matched pair and a rival. A rival who is crazy, who is desperate. A rival whose heart is broken. A shy boy who goes to a school where they teach you how to be a warrior with a gun.

So.

I am still in the shadows behind Ryan Sweeney and the pistol he has pulled (so fast!) from Jorge's holster, where it sat there on the table like a sleeping dragon.

"Stay right where you are!" Ryan yells. He swings the gun back and forth in front of the stage, and when he turns from side to side, I can see the sweat on his face and his hand that is not so steady. "I just came here to see Carmen, that's all. Just her."

He stops talking, his hand on the gun still shaking. The whole room is silent. All we can hear is the sound of cars passing by on the street. I think about trying to sneak up behind him and maybe I can get the gun?

No. He is much bigger and much stronger than me. I glance down at my phone on the table. The sound is off. I reach for it ever so carefully and push 3, my speed dial for Marco, who is working just down the street. Maybe when he sees my number but hears nothing on the voice mail, he will know that something is wrong and come to find us.

Carmen turns around again to face the cadet. She locks his eyes with hers and now she takes a few steps to the side. Ryan follows her with the gun. He begins talking again, pleading with her. "If you say that you'll come with me . . . then nothing bad will happen. I didn't come here to hurt anyone. C'mon now. We'll just walk away. You and me."

I watch helplessly from behind. What can I do? Why is she walking around like that? Is the gun from Jorge's security job loaded? Would he really pull the trigger? I want to shout for someone to help us, but of course, I cannot make a peep. But . . . ah . . . now I see that as long as Carmen is pulling Ryan's attention away from the stage, he is not seeing the guys exchanging looks and Lenny taking hold of his drummer's stick.

My eyes swing back to Carmen, hands on her hips, and at the crazed cadet with the gun. I feel my lips mumble a prayer, and at the same time I see Lenny's arm fly up and his wrist flick the stick across the room and it hits the pistol, which goes sliding across the floor and the stick does, too, and now there are shouts and the guys are running straight for Ryan, who turns to face Lenny like a mad dog and their fists go wild.

I run out from the shadows and over to Carmen. I pull her away and toward the bar, where we stay until at last the fighting and yelling have stopped and there is Ryan on the floor with a bloody face and eyes closed and Lenny standing over him with the gun, and now here comes Marco, too, and Tommie the manager, who yells, "Call the police!" and so, of course, that is what I do.

Part 7

(Three months later)

Didn't I tell you I'd bring you bad luck?

🌺 *Prosper Mérimée, CARMEN*

MAGGIε

She shows me the number written on the check from the recording company, and I have only seen so many zeros on the casino billboards along the highway. She asks me how much is it to pay for my whole college, because who knows how long this good luck will last? And I say no way, Carmen, this is *your* money. I have money put aside from working and I will get a good scholarship and pay for college myself. And for the first time since I can remember, we have a big fight. We are talking angry to each other and cursing and shouting sometimes, and this goes on through the afternoon until it is dark outside and we are tired of ourselves and each other.

Then Carmen, she goes to the window and looks across the street at her grandparents' house, which will soon look so beautiful with new windows and aluminum siding. At the house where fourteen years ago, a beautiful young woman brought her little girl and left her for no reason, and for good, with only the clothes on her small back.

"Maggie." Carmen's voice is very soft and quivery now. "*Mis abuelos*, they are old and frail. At the clinic, they tell me that to hire someone from the home-care agency to take them shopping and to their appointments and to check on them once or twice a day, they tell me this will be at least twenty thousand dollars. I don't want some stranger to do this, Maggie. Soon I will be on tour with Lenny and the band, and we'll be away singing for six or seven months—who knows, maybe even a year. I want you to do it. But I am paying you for this because it is a job just like at Quikmart, and you still have your Vo-Tech classes and your studies, and I am thanking God that you are *mi hermana.*"

And of course, this is fair; this is a good thing for everyone. I do not argue with Carmen. And now we are no longer fighting but instead we are smiling at each other. And then we are smiling and crying at the same time and we are hugging and walking downstairs to cook some rice and beans and to plan when maybe Mami can look in on the Navarros for a few days so I can go to one of Carmen's concerts in New York, and together we will walk down the streets with a song on our lips and money in our pockets.

WILL

Within hours after we heard what Ryan did, the Academy released a statement to the press, reassuring the public, the
parents, the police, and all of their alumni that Ryan Sweeney was
a "rogue cadet," that the incident at Gallagher's Pub was "an
isolated one," and that nothing like it "had ever, nor would ever
again, threaten to stain the school's unblemished reputation."

Ryan didn't stand a chance in court after that. The trial was
pushed up so that everything would be over before fall semester.
The general, who could have intervened on Ryan's behalf, instead
broke off all contact with the Sweeneys and even testified for
the prosecution, citing his concern over Ryan's "increasingly
irresponsible behavior."

I did the best I could for Ry: I testified to his character; I told
the court how much pressure I thought he was under; I even
helped his lawyer get five other guys from A Company to testify on
his behalf. But it wasn't nearly enough. Carmen and Maggie;
Lenny, Nick, and Jorge; the sound guy and Tommie the pub
manager—they were all there that day, and they all swore the
same thing: Ryan came into Gallagher's uninvited and unexpected. He made threats. He held them at gunpoint and

demanded that Carmen come away with him. Even if their stories hadn't held up under cross-examination by the Sweeneys' expensive defense lawyer, it wouldn't have mattered. These days, Big Brother is always watching, and the cameras that Tommie had mounted in the main room and over the bar, those cameras saw everything, and so did the jury when they watched the videotape. Theft and illegal possession of a weapon: *guilty*. Aggravated assault and reckless endangerment: *guilty*. Attempted kidnapping: *guilty*.

Now the only thing I can do for my best friend is to write to him as often as I can. He answers me, too, but his letters are written the old-fashioned way—with pen and paper. Unfortunately for Ryan, no laptops are allowed in juvie.

CARMEN

I thought it would be hard to sleep on the bus, but mostly I am so tired after we do a show that I sleep straight through the night and sometimes also through the morning. Today, though, we have a break—a whole day free to rest and to walk around this little town outside of Denver where we sang on Tuesday to a sold-out crowd. I go shopping for three hours, and then Lenny and me, we hike up a trail in the afternoon and find a little waterfall where we have a picnic and some privacy for the first time since the tour began last month.

We are happy together, Lenny and me. Even when we are tired and working very hard with the band, and even when I am homesick for *mis abuelos* and for Maggie, it is Lenny who makes me feel like I can go onstage every night and sing for all those people who have paid good money to hear us. Lenny knows when to take care of me and when to go away and leave me alone in one of my moods. He does not try to show me off like some pretty doll or to keep me too close all the time like a dog. Lenny understands me, and so far this makes me think I could love him for a very long time.

Tonight we are back on the bus and Lenny is sleeping in the

seat across from me. His hair is swept over to one side, and you can see the scar on his forehead from his fight with Ryan. I have tried very hard to forget that day, but sometimes it comes back clear in my mind: the ride to the emergency room, then all the cameras and microphones and everyone yelling out their questions.

After they stitched up Lenny, and after they took our statements, after all the phone calls and the people from the newspapers and the TV—after that, no one was sure what to do about Saturday. Ryan Sweeney was locked up, our pictures were all over the papers and the Internet, and we were all pretty shaky. But the next night, we had a meeting in Lenny's garage and we decided to go ahead. I took Maggie's advice and I put away my fortune-telling cards. Instead, on Friday night, I went with *mis abuelos* to Mass and said many prayers to Mother Mary: for my family, for Maggie and her family, for truck driver Mike and his sick wife, for the band, for Lenny and me, and *sí*, OK, I even said one for my mother and then for the crazy cadet Ryan Sweeney.

"*Thank you,*" I whispered into my closed hands, kneeling down beside my grandmother in church. "*Thank you for not letting him shoot me or anyone else . . . and forgive me if I brought danger to my friends . . . and forgive him, too, for what he tried to do—amen!*"

On Saturday, Maggie helped me get ready for the show, and she even gave me her favorite earrings to wear for good luck. The new gold dress cheered me up a little, but I was still nervous. Gallagher's was packed to overflowing and those two guys were there from the studio to hear us, just like they said. Lenny wore heavy makeup to cover his bruises and the stitches over his right eye, and Tommie hired extra security, just in case.

As soon as we came out onstage, everyone in the place stood up, and they clapped and clapped for us for I don't know how many minutes. This made me want to cry because I knew that if we sang very good, the two guys from New York, they would give us a recording contract, and we would have to leave these people who were giving us such love and courage. And just this time, I thought about my mother and wished she could hear me sing.

I looked back at Lenny, and he winked and blew me a kiss. We started the first set and I was singing like my life depended on it (which it did), but also like there was nothing at stake and I was in Lenny's oil-can-smelling garage and Maggie was close by studying her flash cards and we would all be young and free forever.

RYAN

The rec hall here isn't that much different from the one we had at the V: foosball, Ping-Pong, card tables and board games, a few nice TVs, couches, and even a pretty good sound system. That's Tyrell Walker over there by the speaker. Rumor has it he was the best DJ in northeast Philly before he got arrested for aggravated assault. So—I guess you could say Tyrell and I have something in common.

"Hey, Walker—kill that hip-hop crap and find us some tunes, will ya?" Lyle McVail yells from one of the couches, where he's been reading the most recent issue of *Food and Wine* for the better part of an hour. (Lyle was a cook's apprentice at an upscale restaurant in Philly. Trouble is, he kept helping himself to leftovers—and to the restaurant manager's safe.)

I shuffle the deck I've been playing solitaire with while my cellmate, Maurice, sits across the table, sketching me.

"Hold still, man," he pleads in the forced-polite way we all seem to talk to each other here at the Central Penn Juvenile Center. "I can't capture your exquisite handsomeness with all your squirmin'," he says, sarcastic as usual. I try not to move while I shuffle the deck again. "I'm givin' you a tattoo on your neck—just for effect," he announces.

"OK," I say. "That's cool. What kind?"

"A rose. My old man's got one and—"

"No rose!" I shout, leaping out of my seat and reaching across the table to grab his pencil. I hold it in front of his astonished face. The guard standing near the doorway spins in our direction, glaring. I lower my voice, trying to regain control of my emotions. "No rose, Maurice, you got it?"

"Yeah. Yeah, Ry-Man. I got it. Look, man, I didn't know you had somethin' against roses. . . ."

I deal my solitaire hand while Maurice completes his sketch of my neck, a small American-flag tattoo on the left side. Tyrell, meanwhile, has found a pop-rock station, and as the guard watches him warily, he dances by himself across the room. The song ends. And then . . . a voice I've heard almost nightly inside my head since I got here:

Take my hand—come with me,
I can take you where you've never been before—
You are my darling red-faced boy.

My neck feels suddenly warm, my heart thuds. I put down the cards, push back from the table, and walk over to the exit. "Can I get some air?" I ask the guard. He looks at my face, and probably thinking I'll puke any minute, he opens the door.

The rec yard isn't large—maybe a hundred feet long and not nearly that wide. But it's empty and it's away from *her*. Sometimes I wonder if I will ever *really* get away from her. Sometimes I wonder if there is such a thing as a spell—if your mind can be overtaken by some outside force, even against your own will, and if that force somehow lingers in your cells until you die. I laugh to myself when I think of this . . . the cruel way things turn out. The way that when you cling to the idea that life is fair, it seems to go to extra lengths to prove just the opposite.

But there is a brighter side to what's happened: My father has refused to visit me and, according to my mother (who does visit as often as she can, and who says she's explained everything to Adam and he pretty much understands), has basically disowned me. It took me all of a week and two sessions with the facility counselor to realize that maybe, just maybe, I might be free to choose my own life once I get out of here. Dr. Greenway (that's the counselor's name) has got me thinking that I really might have a decent future out there somewhere . . . one without the inflexible rules of the military and the inhumanly high expectations of my father.

It'll take some time, I know. I figure I'll have to spend a couple of years, at least, doing penance for my actions that day at Gallagher's. Still, the longer I'm in here, away from all the past pressures, away from the temptation of *her* . . . the more I feel that a new Ryan Sweeney's in the making. One that I can live with. One that has hope for a future in which I make all the big decisions, in which I choose my own goals and the people I want to spend time with. And Will is definitely part of that picture. He's never given up on me, and I know he'll still be my best friend when I get out. He'll always be there for me, and that's another thing I'm thankful for. A big thing.

I stroll aimlessly around the perimeter of the high-fenced yard, looking out through the wire at the still-green hills that in a few short weeks will be tinged with yellows, reds, and oranges. It's weird how it took getting sent to a place like this to set my mind free. I can't say that I'm happy here, exactly. No—that's not the right word at all. But I feel more hopeful than I think I've felt in a long time.

I take a deep breath, feel the breeze on my face as I walk around the far corner of the yard. When I look down again, something catches my eye. I stop. About four paces ahead is a coiled snake, thick-bodied and black, sunning in the short-cropped grass. Instinctively I look around for a rock or a stick but find none. I approach the reptile. As my shadow falls across its body, it instantly uncoils and slithers, effortlessly as water, under the fence.

I watch as it winds silently through the higher grass outside the yard—slick, beautiful, and deadly. For a moment, I catch the scent of smoke mingled with roses.

I watch until it disappears.

AUTHOR'S NOTE

Much like my previous novels—*The Trial, Pieces of Georgia, Kaleidoscope Eyes,* and *Ringside, 1925*—this story has ties to my youth. My parents were avid opera fans, and their vast collection of vinyl records played almost incessantly throughout my childhood. From the twin speakers of the stereo that squatted in our dining room, sopranos, baritones, basses, and tenors belted out songs in a multitude of languages. Of course, I didn't understand a single word they said! But the emotional impact of their voices and the music transcended the language barrier, so that I sensed the tragedy of *Madama Butterfly*; the deception and destruction of *Faust,* and the lighthearted humor of *The Barber of Seville.*

But one opera remained my favorite: *Carmen.* Sung in French (a language I later majored in at Gettysburg College), it was by turns lively, raucous, playful, passionate, dark, and tragic. Over time, I learned that the opera is based on a novella from the mid-1800s by the French author Prosper Mérimée. In Mérimée's tale, Carmen is a wily Gypsy who works in a cigarette factory in Seville, Spain, but lives freely among a group of notorious smugglers and bandits, for whom she is a spy and scout. When a young soldier (Don José) falls hopelessly and obsessively in love with her, he abandons his life of duty and honor and becomes a bandit. Carmen returns his affection for a while, but when he becomes too possessive, she casts him off in favor of a young bullfighter. In a jealous rage, José follows her to the bullring, where he demands her love for the last time. When she refuses, he stabs her and she dies.

For me, Carmen's character represented an altogether different kind of heroine: adventurous, openly passionate, and unapologetically independent—a welcome change from the coy, passive, well-behaved heroines who inhabited most of the fairy tales I read and the TV sitcoms I watched as a young girl in the early 1960s. Though I would be in junior high before I heard the word "feminist" or knew anything about the ongoing struggle for women's rights, I sensed instinctively that Carmen was a powerful female who lived adventurously, made her own rules, and accepted her tragic fate with dignity.

I suppose it was just a matter of time until I wrote my own story based on the original. In doing so, I used Prosper Mérimée's tale more as a loose scaffold than as an absolute blueprint, and I made many decisions regarding how closely I would mirror the original (i.e., which aspects of the plot and characters I would keep and which I would alter, according to the needs of the narrative). There were only a few things I was sure of as I began the book: (1) that Carmen would remain a fiercely independent young woman; (2) that a soldier (or cadet at a military school) would fall in love with her; (3) that his desire for her would consume him and bring about his downfall; and (4) that their relationship would end in violence.

Setting has always been very, very important to me, and so I chose to have Ryan and Will attend the Valley Forge Military Academy, located about twenty miles from my home in southeastern Pennsylvania. And let me be clear: I have nothing but the utmost respect for those men and women who protect our country by serving in the armed forces. The training is difficult, the life demanding, and the sacrifice absolute. As an *author*, however, my duty to the story comes first, and I must put my personal feelings and opinions aside when I enter the heads of my characters. Therefore, in this version of *Carmen*, Ryan and Will wrestle with their own attitudes toward military-school life, with its strict rules, rigid schedules, and expectations of perfection, as well as with the grim realities of the Iraq War. In addition (and again in order to accommodate the characters and the plot), I took fictional liberties with certain details of the VFMA campus, faculty, duties, ranks, curriculum, and daily life.

Further READING, LISTENING, AND VIEWING

Books

Conroy, Pat. *The Lords of Discipline*. Boston: Houghton Mifflin, 1980.

Mérimée, Prosper. *Carmen and Other Stories*. Oxford World's Classics. Translated by Nicholas Jotcham. New York: Oxford University Press, 1999.

Trousdale, William. *Military High Schools in America*. Walnut Creek, CA: Left Coast Press, 2007.

Sound Recording

Bizet, Georges. *Carmen*. London Symphony Orchestra. Claudio Abbado. With Teresa Berganza (Carmen) and Plácido Domingo (Don José). ℗ 2005 by Deutsche Grammophon. DGG B000402902 (two compact discs).

Films

Bizet's Carmen. DVD. Orchestre National de France. Lorin Maazel. With Julia Migenes (Carmen) and Plácido Domingo (Don José). Directed by Francesco Rosi. Sony Pictures, 1999.

Carmen. DVD. The Metropolitan Opera. James Levine. With Agnes Baltsa (Carmen) and José Carreras (Don José). Directed by Brian Large. Deutsche Grammophon, 2000.

Carmen: A Hip Hopera. DVD. Directed by Robert Townsend. With Beyoncé Knowles and Mos Def. MTV, 2001.

Taps. DVD. Directed by Harold Becker. With Tom Cruise, Timothy Hutton, Sean Penn, and George C. Scott. Twentieth-Century Fox, 1981.

Web Sites

www.vfmac.edu (Valley Forge Military Academy and College)
www.nps.gov/vafo/index.htm (Valley Forge National Historical Park)

Selected scene-by-scene synopses of the opera *Carmen* by Georges Bizet

www.allaboutopera.com/opera_synopses.php?opera_ndx=70
www.losangelesopera.com/production/0809/carmen/synopsis.aspx
www.metoperafamily.org/metopera/history/stories/synopsis.aspx?id=117

ACKNOWLEDGMENTS

I am grateful to the following people for providing me with good advice, wise editing, reliable information, and emotional support as I wrote this story: Joan Slattery and Allison Wortche, my awesome editors at Knopf Books for Young Readers; Iris Broudy, a sharp-eyed copy editor; Amy Schroeder, a lynx-eyed proofreader; Alyssa Eisner Henkin, my trusted agent at Trident Media Group; Laura Shovan, a friend and poet; Captain Jason Dickson, a VFMA graduate; Guy and Lori Donatelli, Chester County, Pennsylvania, attorneys; Diane Geis, reference librarian, Chester County Library, Exton, Pennsylvania; and Allison Oberholtzer, Alex Fredas, Leigh Bryant, and Neil Bryant.

A very special thanks to Maribel Castro, middle school librarian, St. John's School, Houston, Texas, for her help with the Spanish culture and language details of this novel.

And finally, my gratitude to the French writer Prosper Mérimée (1803–70), whose novella *Carmen* provided the inspiration for my story, and to the French composer Georges Bizet (1838–75), whose opera *Carmen* filled my childhood imagination with visions of Gypsies, soldiers, and bandits.

Also by Jen Bryant

The Trial
A Bank Street College of Education Best Children's Book of the Year

★ "Extraordinary. . . . As Katie says, 'When a man's on trial for his life / isn't *every* word important?' Bryant shows why with art and humanity."
—*Booklist*, Starred

Pieces of Georgia
A VOYA Top Shelf Fiction for Middle School Readers Selection
An NCSS-CBC Notable Social Studies Trade Book for Young People
A Bank Street College of Education Best Children's Book of the Year

★ "Through Georgia's artwork, noticing details others miss, learning about painters like O'Keeffe and Wyeth, and reaching out to others, the fragmented pieces of this steely, gentle heroine become an integrated whole."
—*Publishers Weekly*, Starred

Ringside, 1925: Views from the Scopes Trial
★ "The colorful facts [Bryant] retrieves, the personal story lines, and the deft rhythm of the narrative are more than enough invitation to readers to ponder the issues she raises."
—*Publishers Weekly*, Starred

"Bryant offers a ringside seat in this compelling and well-researched novel. It is fast-paced, interesting, and relevant to many current First Amendment challenges."
—*School Library Journal*

Kaleidoscope Eyes
A Chicago Public Library Best of the Best Book
An IRA Teachers' Choice

★ "Readers will fall under the spell of the delicious plot."
—*Kirkus Reviews*, Starred

★ "Sincere and well-paced, with the backdrop of a tumultuous period in history, the story is not easily forgotten."
—*Publishers Weekly*, Starred